Ghost
BROTHER

Ghost Brother

SYLVIA SÁNCHEZ GARZA

PIÑATA BOOKS
ARTE PÚBLICO PRESS
HOUSTON, TEXAS

Ghost Brother is funded in part by a grant from the Texas Commission on the Arts. We are thankful for its support.

Piñata Books are full of surprises!

Piñata Books

An imprint of
Arte Público Press
University of Houston
4902 Gulf Fwy, Bldg 19, Rm 100
Houston, Texas 77204-2004

Cover and photo design by Mora Des!gn

Library of Congress Control Number: 2024944279

∞ The paper used in this publication meets the requirements of the American National Standard for Information Sciences—Permanence of Paper for Printed Library Materials, ANSI Z39.48-1984.

Ghost Brother © 2024 by Sylvia Sánchez Garza

Printed in the United States of America
October 2024–November 2024
5 4 3 2 1

This book is dedicated to my loving parents, Joe V. Sanchez and Elida Reyna Sanchez. I love and miss you both very much. Thank you for being an inspiration to me and always believing in me.

IN MEMORIAM

Elida Reyna Sanchez (1933-2019)

Joe V. Sanchez (1932-2021)

Cris

My brother is dead.

I stare at his picture surrounded by candles propped up on the living room coffee table.

"Carlos... what happened?"

He smiles back at me, frozen in time, pale looking with dark, straight hair and blueish eyes that look as if you can precisely pick them up like jewels.

"It could have been you, Cris. You're a miracle," Mamá says.

I guess I should be happy.

I tiptoe into our bedroom, then slam the door. The floor is hard and cold; crumbs stick to my bare feet. Light from the window cracks through the torn curtain. I sit down on his bed as I've been doing every day, hold on to his pillow, trying to embrace the scent. It's not there anymore. I open up my laptop and turn on some music. We like old eighties rock.

"Your dad loves that music," Mom always says.

I strain my ears to listen to Talking Heads, "Once in a Lifetime," and remember the sickening thoughts stuck in my head. I start typing into the Google search engine. *Drag Racing Accident, Malton, Texas*, and several articles come up. My brows knit in a frown, and my laptop screen stares at me, glowing discontentedly. I click on the one that says "Investigation," and nothing. I click again. "Ughhh." It freezes. I slam my laptop shut and stuff it into my backpack. "Dammmmn—internet reception, again."

Nothing ever happens in Malton, at least nothing ever happened until a few months ago on *that* Friday. Most of the time I stay in my room, locked up, reading, typing whatever I can on my laptop to get everything out. I'm using the school's laptop and hotspot. We can't afford that stuff. I immerse myself in books to help me leave this place, at least for a while. Everyone in this town remembers the accident; they just don't want to talk about it.

Our tiny community in deep south Texas is still shaken by the news. It's not a big city, but Carlos and I like it here.

Today, the sun is popping up between the gray clouds. A bright red cardinal sits on the edge of the yard by the oak tree as I walk outside to get the daily newspaper for my mom. I never read it anymore; I'd rather check my phone. She still prefers to see everything in print, even though everyone I know uses their phones for almost anything and everything. I place the paper on our kitchen table and notice that blasted across the front page is, "Police investigate fatal drag racing accident: search for the third car continues." I check my phone. I have text messages from my best friend, Damian, but I don't feel like responding. He wants to know the same thing I do; I know him. Damian practically lives at our house, except lately he's giving me space. My phone vibrates. I stare at it, then silence it. Will we ever be able to forget that day? For me, May 23, 2015, became the worst day of my life. For my brother, Carlos, life ended.

"Talk later," I whisper to the phone without answering it. The sink faucet steadily drips… I stare at it shaking my head.

We need to fix that. Drip, drip, drip. The rhythm stays in my mind.

Everything about Carlos and me was different, from our hair to our skin to playing football. He played; I didn't. If not for my asthma attack a few years ago, I guess I could have played if I wanted to. It just wasn't my thing. We're brothers and in the same grade, and we have always had a bond. As kids, we'd share our birthday celebrations with one cake and a homemade *piñata*. Our grandma always made it and filled it with candy. I never enjoyed beating the uniquely crafted masterpiece into a million pieces. Carlos, on the other hand, was competitive. He kept the shattered pieces as trophies.

Now, Mom meanders around the house, and my father, who I don't even know, wants to reunite. He's been MIA for most of my life. But Mom doesn't want him around. Could he be so bad?

Oh.... and I went back to school a few weeks ago and had to face everyone as if everything was fine. Nothing is fine. Nothing will ever be fine.

Carlos

I stand in the living room next to the old, torn-up sofa. Cris is mirroring me. I'm looking at my football picture. Yep, I scored lots of points for our team. They should have found the one where I'm running with the ball. My hair was longer then and curled up on the ends. That's a good one, but I guess they didn't have time to pick a better one. "Hey, brother. I'm here, CC." Mouthing words, I try to place my hand on his shoulder. When we were kids, sometimes we'd call each other C and CC. I was C and Cris was CC. That was only between us. Now he doesn't have anyone to call him CC.

I gaze out the smudged window at the sky illuminating the cold darkness of night, and I'm overcome by the endless brightness. The summer vanishes like eerie mist, and I hum Pink Floyd. Yes, I'm still numb. My mind is stuck, fragments of my nightmare from that day loop over and over and don't let me sleep. I see myself waking up in a cold sweat, shaking with eyes wide open, only to figure out I can't sleep. How am I supposed to sleep? I guess I don't. If only I had taken the wheel.

Ever since our dad left, Cris thought it was his responsibility to watch after me. Mamá didn't even have to ask him; he just did it. He was always the more responsible one and definitely more mature, I admit. He always helped around the house with the cooking and cleaning and even kept up the yard. Yep, I guess he had better grades, too. I didn't have time for that with football. I was the one meant to do bigger things, any way you look at it. "Don't worry about anything, *m'ijito*. You'll probably be able to get a football scholarship," Mamá would tell me. Well, so much for that.

He picks up my picture, shakes his head and exhales. I see his breath on the glass of the picture frame, and then he sets it back down carefully. He walks into our bedroom, and I follow him. I sit down on my bed and watch him mess with his computer... always studying. Everything is the same. My football is there, my backpack is tossed by the side of the bed. I hated lugging that thing around. Even my guitar is leaning against the wall. I tried playing it, but I never got good enough. Cris was the one with musical talent. He was good at it. He's not one to brag, but he can sing and write music. It comes naturally to him. Mamá used to tell us Uncle Carlos also played by ear. He didn't need sheet music. I guess Cris is kind of like him.

Cris gazes at the screen, clicking on the keyboard. I glance over my shoulder, noticing the curtains moving, and forget for a minute I'm in this other reality. Cris closes his eyes, folds his arms across his chest and leans back. Who is he going to talk to now? Damian has his own issues. How is he going to get through school without me there? He does have that nerd thing going on.

"I'm here," I try to say, but nothing comes out. I've been practicing, but still nothing.

I focus on what's happening and try to piece everything together. I'm getting fragments of what happened, but not everything makes sense. I notice the picture of Cassandra and me by my bed. I do remember Cassandra and the accident. There was an accident. I can't get that out of my head.

I hear noises in the kitchen. Without realizing how, I'm sitting across from Mom. It's as if I have some superpower or something. I can appear where I need to be. It's crazy. She's gripping a cup of black coffee. There's a picture of the Virgin surrounded by red roses on the cup, and the white of her knuckles sticks out more than ever.

"*No llores, Mami. Ya no llores, Mamita.*"

The tears roll off her face and splash into the cup. Sobs and gasps for air engulf her and fill the gloomy room. She rests her head on her crossed hands.

"Don't worry, I'll do something," I try to tell her.

I want to crush or hit something. It's not fair my mom is heartbroken. My body is weightless—*nada*—but I still hurt inside. The truth will come out. I have to find out who was driving the third car. Why was it there? I'll figure it out. If I can get my dad over here, he can help. I know I've seen him, but how do I communicate with him?

It's the night of the end of the school dance and we've all been looking forward to it. Cassandra and I have gotten closer, and who knows what tonight will bring.

"Well, we can't take my pickup. I need to fix the tires, and I haven't had a chance to do it. Besides, it's not comfortable for the four of us. We probably won't all fit in it," I announce.

It would be nice to go in my pickup, though, because I'm always in control whenever I'm behind the wheel. It's my old faithful. Yeah, it's beaten up, but I've worked on it to restore it, and now it's pretty cool. It's nothing like Cassandra's, though.

Cassandra's thick black hair glosses down her back and bounces with the slightest movement. She always pushes it out of her face and then plays with her big hoop earrings. She came from a family much better off than ours, not that they're rich, but we are SNAP poor, and they definitely aren't like us. When we were kids, we had food stamps, but now it's a government card. I guess she is a small step above the dirt poor we are, which is way better. Cassandra's dad bought her a Jeep Cherokee to drive to and from school, and she doesn't even have a license yet. It's used, but still, that's a pretty big deal. She's a bit spoiled, I guess.

The night starts with Cassandra joining us at our house. She's dressed up in a fancy pink dress with matching high heel shoes. Her hair is up in a stylish wrap with flowers in it like a dancer in a Broadway musical. Cassandra is eager for us to check out her Cherokee.

"I'll drive, Cassandra. I don't drink anyway." Cris, as always, tries to be the big brother that he is by a few minutes ahead of my birth.

"The boring brother." Cassandra winks at Cris.

"I like to read—that's not boring," he answers.

She throws her head back, giggling, making her hair bounce up and down.

I smile at her and start to laugh. "Great, then we're set. *¡Dale!* It'll be great!"

Cris, Damian, Cassandra and I all pile inside her car. There's dust covering the dashboard, and the seats seem torn at the edges. Cris has never even driven her car, but is eager to get behind the wheel.

We're dressed up in our best blue jeans and collar shirts. No one knows what the night is going to bring. Everything starts moving so fast. It's just a blur.

"Hold on, Cris!" I yell out. "Stop the car. I forgot something."

The Jeep stops, and I turn and run back inside, yelling back, "Y'all know I can't go anywhere without my jacket."

It was my letterman jacket, the one that my dad wore when he was in high school. Grandma would tell us whenever he'd wear the jacket, he scored a touchdown the next game. And when he wore it, he passed his tests, even though he hadn't studied for them. When *I* wear it, I feel close to my dad. I'm protected.

I slip on the jacket and place my hands in the deep pockets, sliding my fingers across the smooth wooly material. I head back out and yell, "All right, all right, let's go! *¡Vámonos!*"

Mamá steps out into the front yard and waves at us, blessing everyone, signing the Cross in the air, then blows us a kiss. We back up, and she comes up to the Jeep, leans into the window and says, "*Qué Dios los bendiga.*" She reaches in and kisses Cris and then comes around and kisses me. "*Los quiero mucho.*"

I hold my cheek. "Love you too, Mom," both Cris and I say in unison.

We take off with Cris behind the wheel, laughing along with everyone in the car. The cologne and perfume mix, creating a fresh new aroma in the air. I inhale slowly and hold onto the sweet smell of hibiscus mixed with herbal sage and close my eyes for a moment. I'm alive. We are alive. Turning the radio up full blast, I turn to Cris, and we both start headbanging to the beat of Queen, pretending to be Wayne and Garth in *Saturday Night Live!* It is old school, but we love "Bohemian Rhapsody."

The air is crisp, and the evening is gleaming with brightness. There are few cars on the road as we make our way toward the high school. We arrive at the dance and hear the blaring music coming from inside the gym. It's probably not too packed because the parking lot is still kind of empty, and it is already getting late. As we get out of the car, I raise my collar and turn away from the whirling wind.

When we enter the gym, the DJ is playing some blah song, and a few people are on the dance floor with the lights only semi-dimmed. Scents of recent PE classes, baked goods and cologne fill the huge room. Kids are grouped in their designated corners of the gym just like the way they assemble during lunch at the cafeteria tables, only now there's no scent of tater tots or pizza.

We walk past the chaperones at the front door and then past the athletes. They give us a "S'up" nod and keep talking to each other. We walk past the nerds, but they don't even notice us. Then we see Jack, aka, Big J, and Red standing next to the snack bar. They are the only kids in school who send chills down our spines. It's as if they always have a radar on us.

Damian stops. "What the hell are they up to now?"

"This doesn't seem like much of a dance, guys. They're not even playing our kind of music," I say.

Cassandra's face gets long, and she stares at the floor. Then she looks around for some of her friends.

"Let's just give it a chance. Maybe it'll pick up in a bit," Cris says.

"Yeah, fine. I'm going to the ladies' room, *chicos*," Cassandra says, seeking refuge where she knows we can't join her.

"What do all of them possibly do in there all that time?" I ask.

We stand outside the girl's bathroom for what seems hours until Cassandra comes back with glossier lipstick on. She seems better, a little brighter as she takes a seat at a table next to us and a group of our friends.

"Hey, the girls say they'll text me later to see what we're going to do. Maybe they'll join us," she says, looking at me.

"Great!" I say.

"Hey, Cass..." Damian turns to her. "What the hell do y'all do in there for so long, anyway? Is it like a lounge for girls or what? Y'all always come out of there laughing."

"Whatever, Damian. You're clueless." Casandra laughs as she shows her friends a video on her phone, and they bend over with laughter. At least now, she'll give the dance a chance.

I convince Cris and Damian to check out the snacks at the student council's refreshment stand. The popular kids are camouflaged behind a folding table with a handmade poster taped to the edge listing prices. They're selling sodas, chips, hot Cheetos with cheese and whatever else the school allows.

As we approach the stand, Big J and Red show up looking like they woke up one second ago. Big J wears shirts much too tight; they pop open on the sides. He has a scar on his right cheek, apparently he fought some gangster, and they both ended up in jail. One of the mean guys always follows Big J around closely and does whatever he tells him to. His name is Redmond, but everyone calls him Red for short. He has bright red hair and freckles. They act all tough, not at all like most of the other kids. These guys are plain mean.

During elementary school, our teacher made Big J a hall monitor and that went to his head. Ever since then, he's been getting in trouble. Because his dad is the sheriff, he thinks he can tell everyone what to do.

Purposely, Big J bumps right into my back, laughing and spinning to glare at Red.

I jump back and eyeball him. "Hey, *vato*, watch it!"

Damian quickly comes up like some kind of superhero and gets in between us.

"*No te dejes*, bro," he tells me.

"Don't worry. These guys don't scare me," I say acting brave.

Big J barks at us, "Hey, where you guys from? Don't you think you and your friends should go back to the country you came from?"

Red goes along with Big J, copying everything he says and does. He laughs uncontrollably, holding onto his stomach, acting like Big J's hilarious.

"We're from *this* country, just like you," I answer.

"Well, your football player friend here sure isn't," he growls, pointing at Damian and looking him over, head to toe. Shaking his head, he laughs again. "You shouldn't be speaking Spanish here. This is America. We speak English here, dude. Tell your family you guys aren't welcome here."

Big J and Red high-five each other.

I try to keep my cool, but it's hard with this bozo. As calmly as possible, I answer him: "America is a country of many languages. We can speak any way we like."

Big J laughs.

"Yeah, maybe you should make yourselves useful and go pick oranges in our grove. I hear you're pretty good at that," Red chimes in.

Cris looks at me, and his eyes squint, getting small. Wow, so what if we have part-time jobs picking fruit! It's hard work, but we were happy to help out and make some extra cash. This creep probably doesn't even know what hard work is.

"Keep it cool, brother. They don't know any better."

I start sweating, and my heart beats so fast it feels like it's going to jump right out of my shirt. My palms start getting clammy, and now the sweat is dripping down my face. I wipe it away with my arm. The last thing I want them to think is that I'm scared. I'm not. They may try, but they don't scare us.

They purposely bump into Cris and me and make it look as if we've bumped them, when the last thing in the world we want is to pick a fight.

"Hey! Why'd you do that for? You looking for a fight or what, man?" Big J yells at us.

I start to walk away and tell Big J, "Come on, dude, we're not looking for trouble. We're just trying to get some snacks for our friends. Go pick a fight with someone else."

Big J isn't having it. He pushes his huge body forward and presses his pimply, pink face into Cris' soft face so their noses are touching. Cris doesn't even flinch.

"Back off!" I shout.

Big J gestures with his hands, acting like a small child in trouble, "Oh, I'm so scared. What are you, their bodyguard?"

"I'm warning you… keep it up and you'll be sorry," I threaten.

Big J backs up, and Red snickers as they turn around and head toward the dance area, cussing us out while their voices fade away.

Sweat is still dripping down the side of my face. "They're looking for trouble, brother."

Cris stuffs his hands in his pockets and shifts his weight from one foot to the other. "Don't let them bother you. They're a couple of cowards."

I clench my jaw and mumble an obscenity to myself. "No one should talk to anyone like that. It's not right."

I pay for the snacks and nod to Cris. We weave back through the dance floor, searching for Cassandra to see what she wants to do. We find her at a table at the back of the gym, sitting with some of her girlfriends, their arms and legs crossed, staring into space.

She quickly stands up, ready to get out of there. "Finally! Where were y'all?"

"We ran into some of our favorite people, right, Cris?"

"Whatever you say."

The music is not our type at all. They're playing too many slow songs and not enough country, rock or dance songs, so we all decide to leave. At the back end of the gym, we see thugs lurking in the darkness as if ready to attack. Hell, they probably have a gun on them since Big J's dad is a sheriff and all. I wouldn't doubt it if he tries to use it.

Cris looks over at me and then glances across the gym. "You all right, Carlos?"

"They don't scare me. I'm not gonna let them ruin our night." I rock back and forth on the balls of my feet. We decide to leave the dance to go hang out at Cassandra's. She has the coolest house right next to the cemetery. We love it. No one can hear us, and it's private.

As we head out, I glance across the dance floor, and Big J and Red are gone. Forget them. They probably got kicked out. Good riddance.

Outside, a horrible storm is blowing. The piercing wind is thrusting leaves and branches across the high school's front doors. There was no warning. The storm came out of nowhere, imitating an angry hurricane. Rain is pounding, but we brave it out and push through it.

Mrs. Solís and another chaperone come after us and try to stop us from leaving. "Kids, you all better wait before leaving. The storm is powerful and dangerous. You'll get drenched... forget driving in this mess."

I look at her, "Thanks, ma'am, but we'll be fine. We don't mind the rain, and besides, we didn't park that far. Right, Damian?"

"Yeah, that's right, ma'am."

"It'll stop in a minute... it's no big deal. C'mon, guys." I say.

"Wait! It's my moral responsibility as a counselor and chaperone to stop you. It's not safe. Your parents would want you to stay here," says Mrs. Solís, standing in front of the double doors.

She can see we've decided to push through, so she steps aside and sighs, "But… if you won't listen, don't say I didn't warn you."

Cris grabs my shoulder. "Carlos, maybe we should wait it out."

"Grownups always talk that way. We'll be fine." I shout out over the racket of the pouring rain. The thunder sounds as if bombs have been set on top of the school roof, and the lightning is showcasing an artistic display across the sky.

I take off my jacket, cover Cassandra's and my head, then stare at the lines of parked cars. We quickly race toward the Jeep as the rain keeps pounding, drenching our clothes. We splash through the puddles and potholes in the parking lot until we reach the jeep. The downpour is drumming on the car roof and hood.

Cris tries to reason with me. "Shouldn't we wait it out, Carlos? C'mon, let's wait. We shouldn't drive in this deluge. We can't even see in front of us. Mrs. Solís was right. We should've listened to her."

I try to take control and walk to open the car door. "Stop, everyone, we'll be fine. There are hardly any cars on the road. No one is out driving right now. We'll be the only ones on the road. Let's go. *Cálmense, chicos*."

Cris blocks the car door and tries to convince me, "No, we shouldn't.… Let's go back inside for a while."

Cassandra and Damian are soaking wet, pleading for us to stop and go back inside.

Sticking my palm out, I say, "I got it, Cris. Give me the keys."

"I'm the one driving, remember?" Cris holds the keys behind his back.

"I got it, brother," I reassure him and place my arm around his shoulder.

Cris looks at me, maintaining eye contact. "You sure? I'm supposed to drive. That's why I came," he tells me.

Increasing the pitch in my voice, I say, "No, I got it. Jump to the back. Cassandra and I will sit in front."

I want to impress my girl, so I push hard to drive. But Cris has always been the responsible one and decides to drive. That's what brothers do: we take care of each other. Maybe he should've given me the keys. I don't know if it would have made a difference. Cassandra pulls my hand away so I won't insist on driving. She didn't want me to make a scene.

Cris ends up driving. He drives slowly in the relentless rain. It becomes more intense, pounding and drumming against the canopy of the Jeep's roof. The gushes are attacking the windows as if they want to break them open.

Our clothes are completely soaked, and the wetness soaks into the car seats and drips to the floorboards.

I squeeze close to Cassandra in the back seat. Her hair, so sweet, like fresh peach blossoms, wasn't like wet hair or rain; it was pure and perfect. For a moment, I wish it would have been just Cassandra and me. She looks at Cris and gives him a smile.

We approach a blinking red light, and out of nowhere, the headlights of an old TransAm come up right next to us. We can hear the revving sound of the engine as the driver taunts us. All of us know the car. All of us know the driver of the TransAm. It's Big J and Red.

"Let him go, Cris, ¡déjalo!" I plead.

"Forget them," Cassandra says, tightening her grip on my arm.

Big J gestures to us with his middle finger.

Cassandra reaches out and places her hand on Cris' back and looks at me. "Please, Carlos, tell him to ignore them."

My eyes are set on the TransAm. "Leave us the hell alone!" I swear at the losers. I'm not going to let them humiliate us.

Damian yanks my shoulder but stays silent.

My heart starts racing and my breathing gets louder and louder. I can feel the blood building up inside me.

Big J rolls down the window. Rain lashes in. He yells out obscenities, gesturing with his hand. Red is bellowing something beside him, making his own gestures. Even through the pouring rain we can hear their cackling.

"C'mon, you bunch of lowlife illegals," Big J continues taunting us.

Cris turns to me, "We gonna let him…?"

I try to calm Cris down, "Let's go. Let's just get the hell out of here."

Big J revs up his engine, and we try to ignore him. The rain is pounding on the cars, and the darkness seems to speak danger to us. Out of nowhere, headlights erupt in the pitch-black, with only the moon helping to shed light on an approaching pickup truck.

In a blink, we're side by side with Big J's blaring machine, the downpour intensifying. Cris grips the steering wheel, squinting as he tries to focus, and rapidly rotates it. Big J doesn't see anything coming. He's too busy revving his engine and laughing. Red is also laughing, throwing his head back when a pickup slides and slams into his TransAm and smashes it into our Jeep. We swerve out of control, and everything goes black. Pitch-black.

Cris

I shake myself off and turn to check if the others are all right. Cassandra is shrouded in blood, unable to get out of her seatbelt. She shakes uncontrollably, staring at me with big open eyes. I reach for her hand. It's ice-cold. I try to slide Carlos' head off of Cassandra's shoulder.
"Nooooo!!!! Please God Nooooo!!!!"
"Carlos!" I yell, but there is no answer.
Distraught and in pain, I start yelling for help. "Please, someone! Please... HELP!!!"
I try to find my phone to dial 911, but I have no idea where it is or if I can even dial.
People and shadows running... Figures stand around the crushed cars. Lights from the houses close by turn on. After a while, sirens blare louder and louder. A man yells into the car. He tries to open the door, but it's stuck. I have no idea how much time has passed. A minute, thirty?
Isn't help coming? Didn't anyone call 911? Someone should have been here by now, but nothing. Where are the paramedics? Where are the Goddamn paramedics?
"Carlos, don't worry, *hermano*, I'm here. I'll take care of you. Help is on the way! Stay with us, please. Don't you dare

die. Do you hear me? Don't you dare." I swear to God. Oh, God, please! Don't let anything happen to my brother.

More people gather. It's not just our car, but Big J's car is messed up, too. The firemen arrive and start getting us out of the cars. Cassandra cries uncontrollably, gasping for breath. She's trying to do both at the same time. Her beautiful outfit is dripping red.

I'm fading in and out, trying with all my might to take control.

"No, I'm supposed to be taking care of you. I promised I would."

There are people all around us. I notice some of these people don't appear solid, but others do. Are they ghosts? Who are they?

I look over at Carlos, who's completely unconscious in the mangled car, and reach over to try and comfort him. When I turn, I see myself and Damian sitting in blood in the front seat. Damian looks scared. Terrified. He's becoming paralyzed, a statue unable to move or talk. It's a nightmare where we can't run or escape. It's too late.

There's blood all over Cassandra's car. It's seeping into our skin, dripping from the roof and puddling on the floorboard. I totally freak out and try as hard as I can to hug Carlos. He doesn't even notice I'm trying. Is it me or him? My mind is weirding me out.

The blood gushes from his chest, staining his white shirt and nice jeans, falling onto the seat of the car. His feet are still planted on the floorboard with his hands stretched out as if trying to hold someone. Incredibly, his hair still looks almost perfect. His eyes look scary and wide open, like they're stuck.

"Cris, I'm fine. Don't worry. It wasn't your fault. Can you hear me, brother? It's not your fault."

It sounds as if he is talking to me. I swear I can hear his voice clearly.

Tears gush out of my eyes as I realize he's gone, and I was the one behind the wheel. Me, his brother.

"Noooo! This can't be happening...."

"Carlos, listen to me. Please try to listen to me. I'm right here."

It's hopeless. He can't hear me.

"It was me. You told me not to drive, and I didn't listen. How could I have let this happen? Carlos..." I cry out in shock.

I hear the cries and the pounding of the rain on the hood of the Jeep while I sit in my puddled blood. They start to pick up my brother's body and take us into the ambulance. They rush us to the hospital with the screeching siren. The rain is still pounding, pounding, pounding onto the top of the ambulance. Dead, dead, dead.

Carlos

Everything goes black as the rain pounds outside the wrecked car. The pounding doesn't stop. It continues—pounding, pounding, pounding. Inside the car, silence screams.

After a few minutes, Cris shakes himself off and turns to check if we're all right. Cassandra, pale and white, is shaking. Her clothes are splattered with blood, but she's alive. Cris and Damian are fine. They were sitting in the front, and the impact was in the back where I was sitting. The truck came right at me. Cris swerved, but the road was too slippery.

"Nooooo!!!! Please God, nooooo!!!!" Cris is yelling and crying.

I reach over to comfort him.

"Carlos!" my brother yells, but I cannot answer.

I can see Cris yelling but I'm completely overtaken by what is happening to me. It's absolutely amazing. Now people are running. Shadows are all around me. Figures are standing around the crushed cars. Lights from the houses close by turn on. Sirens start sounding louder and louder. A man yells into the car. He tries to open the door, but it's stuck.

It seems as if I'm being wrapped in a warm blanket filled with rainbows. "Incredible! Check it out, guys! Have you ever seen anything as awesome as that?" I feel great! Mesmerized by the beautiful bright light surrounding me. I lift myself up above my twisted, bloody body. I miraculously feel as if my soul is connected to everything, and I understand more than I can imagine. I'm whole.

It was instantaneous. I was having an out-of-body experience, except it was a permanent out-of-body experience, and I felt happier than I had ever felt. I felt a love growing a million times inside of me.

"Cris, don't worry, *hermano*, I'm here. I'll take care of you. Help is on the way!"

"Brother, it's fine. I feel great, probably better than I ever have felt. I don't want to go back."

More people are gathering. It's not just our car, but Big J's car is messed up, too. The paramedics arrive and start getting us out of the car. Poor Cassandra is crying uncontrollably. Cris looks scared. Terrified. The other truck is gone.

"No, I'm supposed to be taking care of you. I promised I would, but don't worry, I will. It's all right, brother. I don't feel any pain. I feel the most beautiful feeling—it's unbelievable."

There are people all around us. I notice some of these people don't appear solid, but others do. Are these ghosts? Am I seeing ghosts? "Whoa, am I d-e-a-d?" Is this what dead is? I don't see the tunnel of light to take me to heaven. I examine my bloody self. I don't feel anything. What is happening to me?

I look over at Cris, who's completely distraught in the mangled car, and reach over to try to comfort him. When I turn, I see myself sitting in blood with my head leaning on Cassandra's shoulder, gushing uncontrollably. That is totally gross. Everyone has to go somehow, I guess. Blood, blood, blood, all over Cassandra's car. Her beautiful pink dress is completely covered in my blood. I totally freak out and try as hard as I can to hug Cris, but I can't. I keep trying, but I can't touch him. He doesn't even notice. I lean over and kiss Cassandra's forehead. She doesn't notice either. I try yelling at them. *Nada.*

Funny, I feel sorry for myself as the blood gushes from my chest, staining my white shirt and nice jeans, falling onto the seat of the car. My feet are still planted on the floorboard with my hands stretched out as if trying to hold someone. Incredibly, my hair still looks almost perfect. Wow, that gel really holds up. I have to admit, the hair looks pretty darn good. My eyes look scary, wide open, like they got stuck that way. I try to touch them with my hand, and it goes right through them.

"Cris, I'm fine. Don't worry. It wasn't your fault. Can you hear me, brother? It's not your fault, CC?"

I try to say it even louder to get Cris' attention, but nothing. Tears are flowing from his eyes as he realizes I'm gone and he'll blame himself because he was the one behind the wheel.

"Noooo! This can't be happening...."

"Cris, listen to me. Please try to listen to me. I'm right here."

It's hopeless. He is too distraught to hear me. Maybe later. Someone has to be able to hear me.

Wow, this is bittersweet. I feel great, better than ever, but no one can hear me or see me. I'm dead. I'm invisible. I guess… I'm a ghost now. I've crossed the thin layer that separates the living and the dead. I wish I would have listened to Grandma more. She always talked about this stuff. Now, how am I supposed to communicate with the ones I love?

"It was me," I insist. "You said we should wait, but I didn't listen. How could I have let this happen?"

"I'm right here. It's me, Carlos. I don't even feel pain. It's amazing, like I'm in another dimension or something. You know, it's like all those superhero comics we always read. I sort of have powers now. Pretty cool, huh?"

I stare at my lifeless self in awe. Wait. I can't be dead. How am I ever going to reunite with Dad now? I was supposed to be the starting quarterback next year and get a college scholarship. Maybe I can fix this. What's gonna happen with my family, Cassandra and Damian? I shouldn't be dead. Maybe Big J... he deserved it, not me. Yep, Big J.

All I hear are cries and the pounding of the rain on the hood of the Jeep while I sit in my puddled blood. They start to pick up my body, and I feel nothing. Paramedics yelling at each other and signaling with their hands put us all in ambulances with red blinking lights. Soon, we're rushing to the hospital with sirens blaring. The rain is still pounding, pounding, pounding onto the top of the ambulance.

I'm back home.

Mamá is waiting up for us to get home. She trusts us, but it's something she has done since we were kids. She can't sleep unless we're home.

The rain crashes on the roof, and she runs from one room to the other, checking for leaks in the ceiling. She grabs the back of her head, standing still as a statue. As I get close to her, I see the hair on her arms stick up, and she rubs it, putting on an oversized sweater she has lying over her bed. She knows. She always said she has a gift. Lying down on her bed with eyes wide open, she starts praying out loud over and over. I sit down next to her.

It isn't long before a heavy knock animates her lifeless body. She heads back to the living room. The knocking continues only louder now. Mamá stares at the door but doesn't want to open it. Then I hear a familiar voice yelling. It's Felix.

"Mrs. Pérez, open the door, please!"

Mamá doesn't want to open it, hoping if she ignores it, maybe there won't be any news, but with all her courage, she opens the door. Her hands are shaking, and I swear I can see her heart pounding through her sweater as she anticipates the inevitable news.

Felix is standing at the screen door with bugs buzzing around him. He's the local police officer, tall, slender and known by all. He is a family friend, and his parents grew up with Mamá. Now here he is, standing on our porch with glossy eyes. We've known him his entire life. Felix has been like a brother to us. He went to the police academy right after high school and became a cop to look after everyone in town. He's devoted to the community. Now, here he stands with his hands holding onto his police cap and his head looking down at the steps while he lightly kicks the floor. Politely, he asks if he can come inside. He sets down his dark blue cap, places his hand on his heart and looks directly into the unwelcoming eyes waiting for news.

"Ms. Pérez, I don't know how to tell you this. There is no way to say it, but I am sooo sorry…"

Mom keeps staring at Felix for about a minute, not saying a word, her expression blank. Then, without warning, she falls to the floor, and Felix quickly grabs her and places her on the cushy sofa. Felix gets his cap and starts to fan her with it to give her some air. After a minute, she comes to. I am standing there with my mouth wide open, trying unsuccessfully to call out to her with all my might. It's worse than those nightmares where a monster chases you and you can't scream. You keep opening your mouth wide open and all you get are tiny silent squeaks. Yeah, so much worse. My mom can't see me, and I am right in front of her.

"*¿Qué pasó, Felix?* Please, *no me digas…*"
"Ms. Pérez there was a terrible accident. I'm so sorry to have to tell you this…"
"Carlos, Cris?"
"Cris is fine. Damian and Cassandra are in the hospital."
"*¿Dónde está Carlos?*"
Felix nervously shifts the weight of his legs from left to right. Squeezing his lips tight, he looks at her straight in her eyes, blinking away the sweat dripping down his face.
"Carlos was killed instantly. I am so sorry."
Mamá is silent for what seems to be hours until wails and shouts explode from her core. Our usually calm community can hear my shocked and heartbroken mom as far as the wind carries. The shattering screams escape through the yard and spread throughout the neighborhood into the darkness of the night, reaching up to the full moon that illuminates the tiny town. Mamá is lying on the sofa like a rag doll, and Felix is fanning her with his hat.
Then without warning, she bursts into, "*¡Ay, Dios mío!* My baby, my baby, *mi Carlos, ¿por qué mi Carlos?*"
Felix sits down on the sofa next to her and hugs her. She is sobbing, but I have no tears. Is something wrong with me? My heart is so broken but the tear ducts are not working. Maybe this is all a terrible dream. A terrible nightmare. My mom's world as she knew it is spinning out of control, and millions of pieces of her son's life are dancing through her head and into mine.
I imagine Cris coming home laughing, walking into the room, sitting down on the bed and telling me how he had a great time. Then Damian would come in with Cassandra and laugh and joke like always. I had a conversation with Mamá a few nights ago about how much me and Cassandra like each other and how we would love each other forever, no matter

what. Now what? What's supposed to happen now? How can anyone go on like this? What if Mamá hadn't stepped outside when we left and kissed us goodbye? Now that's the last time my mom kissed me. I place my hand on my cheek, and it slices through my face as if it isn't there.

"Mrs. Pérez, I need to get something from my car," Felix says and steps outside, leaving the scent of death and devastation behind. He reaches into the backseat of his patrol car, grabs something and returns quickly. He hands her my jacket.

"We found it in the back of the Jeep. Miraculously, not a drop of blood got on it. It's wet, but that's it. I knew you'd want it."

Mom grabs the jacket, wet and cold, and holds it to her chest, rocking back and forth. She kisses it over and over, inhaling my Axe cologne on the collar. "My baby, *mi hijo*."

"I'm so sorry, Mrs. Pérez," Felix says.

I see Mamá and feel so badly for her. All I want to do is hug her. I try to wrap my arms around her, but it's as if I'm hugging air. I feel nothing.

"Mamá, I'm here. Please… I know you can see me…. You're just too upset right now. Listen, I'm calling your name. Please listen, Mamá. I'm standing right in front of you. In time, you will let me in. I'll be here. I'll always be here. Pay attention, Mamá. Focus. There aren't many people who can see or hear me, Mamá. You'll have to come through for me. Please focus!"

Felix continues to explain, even though no one seems to be listening.

"He was riding in the back with Cassandra when it ran into a stop sign, trying to avoid an oncoming truck. The rain was coming down hard. It was so unusual, the rain was so strong right at that time. It was like a hurricane. They must have slammed on the brakes and swerved to avoid hitting someone and hit the backside of the car where they were sitting. Cris was driving."

It's hard for him to deliver the news, especially about me. I'm like a brother to him. Poor Felix. He has a tough job.

"Felix! Felix!" I yell at him. Nothing.

"What? Cris driving? Carlos wasn't driving? Cris was driving? I thought Carlos was going to drive. That doesn't make any sense. It wasn't even his car.... Why would he be driving? He wasn't supposed to drive."

"That's not all, Mrs. Pérez...."

"What do you mean, that's not all, Felix? What else can you tell me? How much worse can this get? You just told me my son is dead."

"It appears as if Cris was racing. The driver in the other car also died, and the passenger is in critical condition. I'm sorry."

"No, you're mistaken. My Cris doesn't do anything like that. He's a good boy."

"I don't know... You know how boys are. They do things on the spur of the moment. Their plans change.... Who knows? All I know is Cris was driving."

Mamá turns toward me as if she can see me and stares right into my eyes.

"Can you see me, Mamá?"

I reach out to try to comfort her, but she looks back at Felix. "No, Mamá," I try to say. "We weren't racing. Big J wanted to race, but we didn't do it. We didn't do anything wrong. It wasn't Cris' fault, Mamá." I want to hug her, and I try. Nothing happens. It feels so weird to be inside my own house but not able to comfort my own mother, not be able to touch anything. Being dead sucks.

I glance around, and everything is exactly the way it was when we left for the dance. The bedroom I share with my brother still smells of our Axe cologne. I'm in there looking at the books we left on the bed. Cris loves reading. He read *Rain of Gold* dozens of times, and don't even start me on the poetry. Me, I stuck to the assigned stuff. I can still hear Felix talking to Mamá right outside the room, when I clearly hear someone calling my name.

"Hey, you, Carlos, right?"

What? Someone's actually talking to me. I have to find out who it is.

"Who is that? Can someone see me?"

As I focus, I can see a transparent figure at the doorway of my room, and it scares me.

I stand up to get a better look at him. He seems to be about my age and a pretty big guy, but he's smiling at me. He's wearing a dress shirt a size too small and blue jeans with boots. Could it be? No, of all the spirits in the afterlife, my luck is that my favorite bully is following me.

I slam my fist on the wall, and it goes right through, "Hey, are you…"

As soon as I start to ask him something, he evaporates into thin air. He's gone.

"Where'd you go? Come back here. You know I saw you, right? That's right, run away."

Two other figures start to reappear faintly. One was the same one from before and the other looks familiar. He looks like my uncle. How do they know each other and what do they know?

"Why are you here?" I ask.

No answer.

For now, I need to focus on my family. They need me. Mamá is falling apart, and I don't know what's going to happen to Cris. They better not get the police involved. It wasn't his fault, but if Big J's dad is anything like him, then he's going to turn things around to try to blame Cris. I'll have to help him. I can save him.

I find myself back in the living room.

"You can come with me, and I'll take you to the hospital to see them. Damian's family will be there, too," Felix tells my mom.

"No, I don't want to see him. I don't want to go," Mamá says.

"We have to go. You'll have to identify Carlos."

She smacks her palm over her forehead, "How can a mother be expected to do this, *¿Cómo?* I'm not going to see him, not like that. I won't."

"Mrs. Pérez, I know you don't want to, but this is something you have to do for your son. You have to do it for Carlos. He needs you to do this for him. Besides, you have to be there for Cris. Think about him."

Mamá picks up her head and pushes back the flood of tears. "Cris… how could he have been driving? Tell me it's not true, is it?"

"I'm ready, let's go." She follows Felix out to the police car in the dark moonlight, soaked from the heavy rain.

"I don't want to see him. *No puedo, no puedo, no puedo, Dios mío… ¿Cómo lo puedo ver así? Mi Carlos, mi vida.*"

Felix opens the back door of the police car as the sounds of the radio from police headquarters can be heard muffled by the rain pounding on the hood and windshield. Mamá slides in, and they ride to the hospital with her face buried in her hands and tears splashing onto her lap.

As they arrive at the hospital, everything becomes all too real. The automatic double doors with the red emergency letters written on them instantly open, and the ice-cold draft hits their faces with the faint smell of bleach. There are rows of chairs stuck together with metal armrests filled with nervous and anxious people waiting for news of their sick loved ones. A few people huddle together in the hard metal chairs covered in blankets to protect them from the freezing blasts of air attacking them from the vents inside the unwelcoming waiting room. There's a blanket on the floor with some children lying down watching a big screen TV mounted to the wall. They laugh as reruns of *Sabrina the Teenage Witch* play with Salem the cat talking.

Signaling Mom, Felix says, "Please wait for me here. Let me find out where everyone is."

A police officer walks over with another family and sits them down in a separate area of the waiting room. The lady, who is apparently the mother, is beyond tears and appears to be moving as if in a trance. A man who I guess is her husband and a young girl comforts her as they sit on the cold metal seats. Wait a minute. I recognize that man. He's Big J's father. He's like an older version of Big J, only he has a badge and a gun.

The mother is about the same age as Mamá. I walk over to them because I feel bad for the mother, even though I don't know them. She must be hurting so much. The little girl must be about five years old. I never had a sister, so I have no idea what little girls are like. She looks up at me and smiles. I turn around to see if she's smiling at someone else, but there's no one else behind me. She looks away.

I make myself appear right in front of her and try to wave hello to her. She waves hello to me. I can't believe this.

"Can you see me? Can you actually see me, little girl?"

Nothing. She says nothing. She only smiles at me. I try again, making peek-a-boo faces at her. She laughs.

"I'm Carlos. What's your name?"

"Angie," she says and hugs her mom.

Across the room, I see Mamá getting up and following Felix, so I follow them.

Cries are heard throughout the hospital and escape through the automatic door into the parking lot. Death is everywhere on this somber night, but I know it isn't that. I'm not dead because I'm still here. How can I be dead if I'm here in the hospital? Maybe it's a new life. A different life. If it's a new life for me, it means it's a new life for others, too. I don't know where they are, though. Maybe they're not stuck here like me. It's too soon to know. It's all too fresh. I'll find out where he is.

Hell, it's going to be a new life for everyone. Everything changed in a second. We'll just need to figure out how to communicate with each other.

Felix then goes over to the desk and talks to the receptionist and then turns back to look at my mom, pointing her out. He then points over to Big J's family and also to Damian's family. The nurse looks over at them, nods and then walks away.

A cold chill with goosebumps comes over Mamá as she sits down again and waits. Her shivering body moves rapidly in uncontrolled motions. She wraps her sweater tightly around her folded arms.

"I can feel him." She straightens her back up. "He's with us. He's here."

Cris

Mamá shuffles into the living room, dragging her worn slippers. It's been three months since the accident. Her tangled hair is a wiry nest shooting out in all directions. Her bony fingers claw at the waistband of her faded jeans to yank them up. She'll need to adjust the safety pins again. It looks like she's lost another five pounds. This skeleton that once danced at the slightest hint of a rhythm can't even walk correctly. One foot slides to the side. She reaches out and grasps the mantel, where three crosses and a photo of my brother stand behind a dozen flickering candles. The flames burn day and night; the shrine she built for Carlos never goes dark.

For now, it's only the two of us in our tiny home. I'm hoping my dad will come back, but I know Mamá will never allow him to. With Carlos gone, I need my father. I have so many questions and I know he can answer them, if I can only find him. My grandma is coming to stay with us, though; she's worried about Mom. Most people call her a *curandera* or spiritual healer, but to me, she's Grandma Blanca. "She has special powers, don't ever upset her," Mom always warned us. All she has to do is look at someone right in their eyes or say a specific prayer, and weird things start to happen. But when she smiles at me, beams of sunshine illuminate the sadness, and that's what I want for Mamá.

I'm glad school started a few weeks ago, but it's almost impossible for kids to understand. No one understands that Carlos, my brother, is not there. I don't want to be there either. They brush past me in the halls and whisper. Yesterday, a kid in my second-period class came up to me and said, "Hey, is it true you were drag racing and now your brother's dead?" Then he shook his head and walked away mumbling to himself. Like laser beams, eyes are fixated on me and people whisper as I pass bodies in the halls.

I lowered my head and rushed past the faceless kids. Escaping, I rushed out the back door that led to the student parking lot. I stood against the hard wall with my arms wrapped around my body until the second bell rang.

I can't deal with so many rules—not the school rules, the kids' rules. There are so many things to remember. Do this, don't do that, wear this, don't wear that. I can barely move. These invisible rules are all about cliques, social status and fake friends. You try to fit into one group, and they like you, then the next day they hate you. It's like I'm inside some new level in a video game, and I don't get it. Carlos played football like my dad. He even looked like him. He fit in. But me, I'm an outcast.

In the morning, I force myself to get up, get dressed. Looking at the twin bed in my bedroom, I imagine my brother smiling and grabbing his backpack. "You're gonna be late," I hear him saying. I step outside into the front yard. The piles of crinkled leaves swoosh up in a swirling dance in front of me as I turn on the water hose. I'm the one who takes care of the yard, but I haven't had the energy.

Damian's mom took two plants to the funeral. She placed one next to the casket, and turned to the first pew, where I sat with Mom and Grandma and handed the other plant to me.

"*M'ijito, Carlos estará siempre contigo. Que esta sea un recuerdo... el cariño no muere.* One for you and one for your brother. Take yours home and take care of it, *m'ijito*. This will remind you of Carlos' love. It will grow and make your yard bright," she said to me. Then she turned to look at my brother, displayed in front of an audience, front and center.

Carlos was dressed in his high school football jersey, a fake half-smile on his face and his letterman jacket draped across the edge of the coffin. One by one, everyone came up to tell him goodbye. I don't think he would have liked being there with all those people staring at him and dripping their tears onto his jacket. He didn't even look like himself, with makeup on his face and strange puffy cheeks. I looked around to see if any of the blurs in the pews could possibly be my dad, but *nada*. I'm sure I would recognize him. Mom says he looks like us.

The director came up to me and my mother. "It's time to leave. I'll give you a few minutes to say your goodbyes, let me know if you need anything from the casket, I can help you before we close it."

Then, he stepped back, and we stood in front of Carlos, inhaling the incense and floral aromas mixed in with the floating hints of *pan dulce* and coffee.

"*¡Ay, Dios mío!*" my mother groaned as she threw herself over Carlos' cold body and let out the loudest scream yet: "*My baby! ¡No te me vayas!*"

I knew this was going to happen and, sure enough, Grandma joined in on cue shouting, "*mi Carlitos,*" and fainting on the kneeler in front of my brother.

I stepped up and lifted Grandma up and sat her back down on the front bench. Damian's mom brought her water and a box of tissues.

I went back to the front with Mom and said, "Mamá, I'm sorry. It's time. We need to go. You can't stay here anymore. Say goodbye."

I stepped back to the casket, kissed my brother on the forehead and whispered, "I know it's you. You just don't look like you, bro. If you can hear me, I'm sorry, C. Maybe you did get the scholarship and are playing football in heaven."

"The jacket. Get his jacket, Cris," Mom reminded me, then turned back to call the funeral director standing at the back of the room. "Please let me keep his jacket. It belonged to his dad."

He quickly approached the casket, gently reached for the jacket and gave it to my mom. She held it and sobbed into the sleeves, crying out for Carlos loud enough for my inner core to vibrate.

Back in my front yard, I notice the ivy Damian's mom gave me. New green is unfolding from the vine like paper origami. Looking at the shiny leaves, I half-smile. The plant is much bigger now and is starting to wrap itself around the old oak tree that reaches up into the gray sky.

"I'm going to take care of you, don't worry. You won't die." I whisper to the green leaves as if they understand me.

I have Carlos' old Chevy pickup now, so I drive to Damian's. I'm a sophomore now, but I've had my license since last year. I wish I didn't have it at all.

Damian throws his overstuffed backpack and football gear into the back of the pickup and gets in. "You all right, dude?" He's a DACA kid and hoping for a college scholarship.

Damian appears "tough" with the football players, but with me he's just himself, my best friend. Besides me, he's the only person who knows everything about Carlos. He's practically a brother to us. Yep, he gets kind of annoying at times, and I make him go home, even though he hates being at his apartment because his family is never there. His parents work two jobs to help him and his older sister, Sarah. Even she has a job working at a local packing shed in order to help out.

I glance over at my friend and answer, "*Más o menos.*" I raise my eyebrow.

"Things will get better," Damian says. He reaches to mess with the radio station.

His family's applying for a US visa and goes to court every so often to check on the status. His family moved here from Mexico for a better life.

Damian flips back and forth between songs and finally settles on Garth Brooks' "Rodeo and Juliet." Moving with the rhythm, he rolls the window down and sings along. "You know—I miss him too."

Few people know anything about his legal status. We never cared, but when Big J found out, he started harassing him. Carlos and me had Damian's back, though. No one was going to mess with him.

The problem wasn't exactly Big J knowing. It was Big J's dad, Mr. Tanner, the sheriff. He was mean and had a gun always on his hip and ready for any encounter. We didn't know how he found out about Damian, but he did.

Damian takes a breath and asks, "Did you hear the news that they're searching for the third car? What do you think?"

I ignore him and the sore subject. The sound of the engine rumbles as my legs start to twitch. I push my hair back and take a deep breath as we park in the student parking lot.

The halls become a crazy carnival with kids yelling and shouting and running. I shuffle through shoulders hitting my backpack. It's as if I have some invisibility power.

Damian gestures and heads on toward his first class. "I'll catch up with you later."

I rush through the hallway, hearing footsteps in front and behind me fading quickly as I go through the motions. I don't talk to anyone. I wander into the bathroom, hide in the stall. I hear voices come in, joking and laughing. I stay quiet. The sounds disappear, and I sneak out, look in the cracked mirror, throw water on my face and force a smile. I step back out into the hall and look down at my scuffed work boots, when someone bumps into me head-on. I'm about to explode into a WHAT THE #$@&%*, when I see her.

"Sorry."

I look up, pursing my lips. Standing in front of me is a slender, dark-haired girl with a heart-shaped face. I've never seen her before.

I hand her a sheet of paper I picked up from the freshly waxed floor. "You dropped this."

"Thanks." She looks at the computer printout, clenching it firmly with white knuckles, and then back up at me. "Hey, do you know where room 101 is? I'm sort of new here," she says in a shaky voice with a slight southern accent.

Bodies are pivoting around us as we interrupt the flow of the traffic.

"Ummm, I'm heading there," I say without thinking.

"My name is Selena. Well, actually, it's Lilly Selena, but I go by Selena. Like… Quintanilla, not Gomez. I've never liked Lilly. Everyone here seems to be too busy to talk."

We steer our way through the packed halls until we get to the classroom.

Inside, I find an empty seat at the back of the room. The desks are in perfect rows placed strategically on the white tile floor with a teacher's desk at the front. Zero creativity. My new friend follows me. We sit quietly while everyone around us laughs and jokes.

Mrs. Jenson comes and takes her designated spot at the front of the room. She goes over some of the assigned books—*To Kill a Mockingbird, The Great Gatsby, Lord of the Flies, Animal Farm, The Scarlet Letter.* She acts as if we care about her lesson.

"Class, I hope all of you read your assigned books over the summer," she says. "Your first essay is due next week."

Selena leans over to me. "Did you read any of those?"

I nod.

"Cool, a scholar." Scooting up closer to my desk, Selena grins, looking at me as if she's the Cheshire cat.

"Reading and music are what saved me this summer."

Sighing and glancing up at her, our eyes lock. Her silky hair smells like freshly picked strawberries.

"Saved you? From what?" she whispers back.

"Nothing."

"Excuse me, Mrs. Jenson?"

The entire class freezes and turns toward the door, where Mrs. Solís, one of the school counselors, stands with a forced smile decorating her face and one hand behind her back.

"Can I borrow Cris, please?"

She looks around the class as Mrs. Jenson answers with an annoyed look, scrunching her forehead.

I squint at the walls, still bare. Jenson hasn't bothered putting up any posters or decorations yet. Don't teachers usually do that to make the kids feel welcome? Well... borrow me? What am I, a library book or something?

"I'm sorry. We are in the middle of class. Can this wait? I'm teaching here!" she says, obviously annoyed.

"It'll only take a minute."

Looking back at us, she calls out. "CRIS! CRIS, Mrs. Solís needs to talk to you!"

Not sure who I am, she glares right through me, and I stare right past her wrinkly forehead.

I knew this was coming, not that I care. I have no desire to talk to her. Slowly, I stand up as the whispers begin, and all of the empty eye sockets follow me as I exit the room and walk into the hallway. Mrs. Solís is still standing by the door with one hand in her jacket pocket and the other holding up a newspaper. She's nodding up and down, blinking rapidly. Does she want to interrogate me or what?

As we begin to walk away, she says, "I wanted to check on you. Our school district is here for you—please know that. If you want to talk, come to my office, or let my secretary know. She'll make an appointment for you. How are you doing?"

Mrs. Solís knew Carlos, and maybe she's sorry, but I don't want to talk to her. Why should I? She's silent for a moment and places her hand gently on my shoulder.

"Sure, thanks." I nod and start walking back to my classroom.

"Cris, wait. I've seen the news articles. You know about Big J, right?" she says with an upside-down smile.

After how he treated us? I squeeze my eyes together and bite my lip.

"I'm starting group sessions for those involved in the accident or anyone grieving from the losses, in case you want to join. You might feel more comfortable with your friends," she adds.

"I'm good."

I turn to make sure she's walked away, then pinch my arm. It's the way I deal with pain. When something hurts, I pinch my arm as hard as possible so I can focus on that pain instead of whatever is bothering me. I lean back on the wall next to our classroom door and exhale loudly. Then I slip back into class.

The empty eyes devour me again as I walk to my desk. Selena tilts her head and looks at me, smiling. She's doodling strange symbols on her notebook. I glance at them, and she quickly covers the page.

English class doesn't come to an end soon enough. The kids start picking up their backpacks from the floor and stuffing them fifteen minutes before the bell to be ready to jump out of their seats.

Mrs. Jensen blocks the doorway to hand out a paper about our assignment. "Remember, start working on your essay, kiddos!" She blah, blah, blah, blahs.

As the herd walks out, they start to cluster in the hall around a poster announcing: BACK TO SCHOOL DANCE, SATURDAY.

I overhear some of the kids from class talking about the dance. I guess it's a big deal because where we live, there isn't much to experience except maybe family gatherings and the occasional festival. We don't have a movie theatre or clubs close enough, like other cities do.

Some of the student council kids are standing around with tickets.

One of the organizers yells to the crowd, "Everyone is going to be there. We're hiring a new DJ with a crazy light show and a photographer with a photo booth. Don't miss it!"

"Wow! Not bad for a new school," Selena exclaims. "It's not what I expected, but I'm willing to give it a shot."

I stare at her. I open my mouth to say something but nothing comes out. She smiles until finally, I blurt out, "Perfect! This is just what we both need." Did I say that out loud?

"Both?" Selena picks up her frame glasses and adjusts them onto her nose. She then undoes her ponytail and shakes her head, making her look like one of those models you see in TV-car commercials.

"Well, *I* need this. Plus, it'll give me something to talk to my dad about," I say sarcastically.

"Yeah, I don't want to talk to mine either. Dads can be weird, right?"

"Yep..." I gaze down at my boots and kick the floor. I pinch my arm without anyone noticing.

Selena drops it, thankfully. "What did that lady want?" She holds onto the strap of her backpack.

"Oh, nothing. Oh, hey, do you want to sit together for lunch?" I say.

The light from the windows glistens on her hair and makes it sparkle.

"Okay," she says and goes to her next class.

Selena holds onto her lunch as she and I walk through tables of flat, empty faces. "I sort of met some of those in the girl's bathroom," she says. "They get the award for *Most Friendly*," she adds sarcastically.

I raise my eyebrows.

"They make me feel like such an outsider." She exhales loudly.

Trying to change the subject, I ask, "So, how long have you been here in Malton?"

"We've lived here a long time, but we recently moved into a different home. You know, the house by the city cemetery?" Raising her forehead, she smiles.

My water bottle falls out of my hand, and I shake as I bend over to pick it up.

"Yeah, my mom's friend, Jack, had some connections. Cool, right?" She tosses her head back and flips her hair like a fashion model.

Chills come over me, making the hairs on my arms stick up.

The emo kids capture our attention as the best bet to fit in since they are dressed in all black and seem to be the most accepting of outsiders. Cool artistic tats cover their arms, and hoodies hide their soft faces. Most in tune with the spiritual world, these kids can actually see us, hopefully even talk to us. No need for a table, they just get comfortable on the floor and lie on each other's laps. Maybe they're like us?

I look at Selena and she agrees. We both kneel down on the cold floor and set our lunches down.

Carlos

The morning of the first day of school, I saw Selena. Cris doesn't know, but I'm still here. I can be at school, at home, even at Selena's house. Yes, I know about her. For some reason, I ended up at her house that morning. I can't understand why her energy attracted me. It was a strong force.

Her face was beaming, and she was pacing around her room like a kid getting ready to celebrate their own birthday party.

"My mom finally agreed to let me enroll in the local high school. I have a new outfit and my driver's license, so I get to borrow the car. So far, so good, as long as I don't get into trouble like last year."

She's talking on the phone with someone and sitting on the edge of her bed making eye contact with Kurt Cobain. He's thumbtacked to the wall, frozen.

"I haven't been able to sleep at night, waiting for the sun to come up," she says and hangs up the phone. Hurtling out of bed and into her bathroom, she tells herself, "Don't overdo it."

While the shower is running, I wait on the bed. She didn't see me, but I didn't try. Maybe she can get through to Cris. I don't want to scare Mom and Grandma. They're emotional right now. I can't get through to them.

She must have some special ability, like Grandma. I can sense it in her energy.

Selena was worried about fitting in at school. I get that. I know what it is to be an outsider. Look at me now. Talk about being an outsider!

Selena pops out, dressed in a short skirt and dark top. She's back on the phone. "I've been here. I do have friends, if you want to call them that, from my mom's church. They're the only ones Mom and Jack allow. Well, the plays and rituals at least are fun. I'll call you back."

Her mom comes into the bedroom interrogating her like a security guard or the wardrobe police. "Are you going to wear that?"

"Oh no! Here we go again. Give me a break, Mom!"

Her mother stands at the door wearing an oversized robe, her hair sticking out all over the place. She points her red, chipped nail at Selena's short skirt.

Selena pulls down her black sweatshirt to try to cover her tummy and sticks her hands in the pockets of the short skirt. "What's wrong with this? I like it and it's comfortable."

"No ma'am, absolutely not. You better change. We don't want you to give the wrong impression."

"Maybe I do. I mean, I don't care about impressions."

Yeah, you tell her. I stand next to her cheering her on.

"Don't start with me," her mom says as she walks toward the closet.

Selena rolls her eyes.

"Look at all these nice clothes you have," her mom says, sorting through some outfits in Selena's closet. "Wear something else," she orders as she walks out and heads to her own bedroom.

Looking at herself in the mirror, Selena smiles, then grabs her backpack, purse, keys and special extras from her medicine cabinet. Then, just in case, she pulls an oversized sweater off the hook of the door and runs downstairs, skipping the last two steps. Rushing out of the musty house, Selena gets into the white, compact car and pulls out of the driveway.

I sit in the passenger seat.

"See ya, Mom!" She waves as she drives away. "The world is waiting for me, and you can't stop me."

Selena pulls into the parking lot at school, and I see her hands start sweating. "Maybe I shouldn't be here," she says, beginning to doubt herself.

I see kids coming and going, laughing and joking around. Why am I stuck in this limbo? I try to shout out at them. No one hears me.

Selena turns toward me. "Is someone there?" She looks around and stares right at me.

"Can you hear me, see me?" I ask.

She smiles and lifts her eyebrows. I knew it.

"How am I going to blend in not knowing anyone here? Don't worry," she tells herself.

Selena looks at her sweater and stuffs it into her backpack. She looks up at the sun, bathing in its glory.

Kids are parking their cars, and buses are unloading students by the dozens. Engines are roaring.

She walks into the school and over to the bustling main office. The seats are all taken, and there is a line to talk to the office staff. She waits. No one notices her. She feels invisible.

"Excuse me," she says, addressing the stranger in front of her. The student looks at her straight in her eyes, scrunching her nose. Suddenly the random stranger grabs her stomach and leaves before getting to the front of the line.

She smiles. It's finally her turn, and she asks for her schedule. The nice lady hands her a printout.

"You have English first period," the office assistant says.

I glance at the computer screen with Selena's information. Under emergency contacts are two names. The one that catches my attention is Rico's name. That's Dad. Why is he listed on her file? I knew she was my key to finding out about him. Cris has to find out.

"Yeah, they sent me the reading assignment this summer. Thanks."

"Do you know where your class is?" she asks.

"I'll figure it out, thanks."

The assistant goes back typing on her computer.

With her schedule in hand, Selena walks out into the hall. She spots the girls' bathroom and makes a mad dash in there for a breather. There's a clique of girls swarmed around the small mirror, fixing their makeup and giggling, acting like they own the place. They stop and stare at her.

"Hi," she says.

Nothing. They stare at her some more.

She covers her stomach with both arms and bends over, sweat dripping down her face as she grimaces. Her body heaves as if she is going to throw up. I didn't see her eat anything—what can she upchuck?

The girls turn their backs to her and keep applying their glossy lipstick.

Selena goes into the last stall and sits down, looking at her schedule, trying not to cry. Her mouth is salivating, and she wipes it with her hand. I know what that means. She tries to hold it back. The last thing I want is for these awful girls to hear, and then it'll be all over the school.

The talking and laughing finally fade away as they leave the restroom. It's quiet now. And then it happens. All is released with excruciating force in a second. Selena takes a deep breath. She walks out and faces the mirror. She splashes water on her red face, washes her hands and rinses out her mouth.

"I can do this." She tells herself. She opens her backpack pulls out the sweater and puts it on.

"There. At least my sweater will protect me."

She pushes up her glasses, straightens her skirt and heads out into the madness. "I'm going to try my best to be friendly. I don't care what those girls think of me."

She reads the printout again. It says, "English II Rm 101."

Elbows and shoulders keep bumping her as she walks looking up at the numbers on the room doors. Students are rushing past her, slamming lockers as if they're dying to get to their classes. *Crash!* Someone has bumped into her. Her printout and purse fly to the floor, and everyone tramples them carelessly.

"Sorry," a soft voice says. A boy is bending down and picking up her printout and handing her the trampled purse.

Selena tilts her head up to look him in the eyes. So much for thinking no one cared.

Later in the afternoon, Mamá is in the kitchen sitting at the table wearing her big, fuzzy robe and slippers. Her eyes are swollen red, and she has a pile of tissues in her hand. She hasn't been at the elementary school lately. She always loved working there, serving all the kids at the cafeteria. They all knew her.

"Do you think we should call Grandma?" Cris asks. "She can come to help us through all of this. With Carlos gone and you losing weight and all... I'm worried about you. I think we need her help. She'd want to."

"No, *m'ijito*, we'll be fine." She forces a smile and adjusts her posture.

"Mom, there's a dance Saturday. Maybe I can get a new shirt to wear. I know we can't afford one, but I'll work to pay for it. I'm gonna start looking for a job. I have some time after school. There are lots of new kids at the school this year. I just want to fit into some group, somehow. I don't want any of them to look down on me, you know, feel sorry for me."

I stand next to my brother and try to get his attention, but he doesn't notice me.

"Groups? You don't need to fit into a group. You fit in anywhere, *m'ijo*. But I know what it's like not to fit in. That's been my life, not fitting in here or there. I get you. *Y te miras tan chulo, mi amor, con cualquier camisa.*"

"Whatever, Mamá. Things are different now. It's not the same as when you attended school. Believe me, it's not the same, but a nice shirt would be great. I'm going to wear Carlos' old jacket too.

"*La* letterman jacket? Are you sure you want to wear it?"

"Yeah, you have it, right?"

Our dad treasured his letterman jacket. I get it. He earned it playing football. Cris never cared for football; that's why Mamá told me to wear it.

"You boys have a lot of your dad in you," she says.

Yeah, but where is he now? I know he's tried. At the funeral—he was there—they didn't see him because he didn't want to be seen. He was off in the distance by himself, wearing black sunglasses. I saw him. He goes by the cemetery and sits on the hard concrete sidewalk and sometimes leaves a flower. His eyes are also dark and heavy, like Mamá's. It has to be him. He looks like me.

Mamá knows. She should tell Cris where to find him. He needs to know the truth. I snuggle up next to Mamá's ear and repeat over and over to her, "Tell Cris Dad works at the diner."

Mamá gently hugs Cris. "*M'ijito*, I didn't want you to know this, and I don't know why I'm telling you this. Your dad works at the diner. I think he's the manager. That's all I know. Please don't be mad at me. I want to protect you."

If only things had started out differently that Friday. I do remember what happened. It wasn't Cris' fault. I need to let him know that, and Dad can help. He cares, he has to. Why was he never around when we were younger? I see moments as if I'm living them, and now I swirl back into a weird place, and it's as if that terrible day is happening again.

For Cris, the stars were lining up, and everything was going well. He knew in time he would see our dad, and everything would be perfect. That was his goal. He wanted to reunite with him. In his mind, he had come up with all kinds of reasons as to why Dad had left. He often told me.

One of them was that he was being held hostage by a mean drug lord, and if he attempted to escape, he threatened to kill his family. Another reason was he had been in a terrible accident and hit his head, resulting in amnesia, and he couldn't possibly remember who his son was. The other one he thought of was he went to work in Mexico, and he wasn't allowed to enter the United States again.

None of the reasons were because he didn't care about us. None of them were because he didn't love us. They were all because he had no choice. It was because he wanted what was best for his children. He did what any parent would do. It was a sacrifice. Cris didn't hate him for it. He didn't blame him. Neither did I.

"Don't do this to yourself," I try to tell Cris.

I follow him around and try my best to yell into his ear, but nothing. He's not listening. Although, sometimes it seems as if he hears me. He'll lift his head, look up and stare into space with a blank expression on his face. I know I'm getting closer. Someone must hear me, see me. You see things like that in movies all the time.

Friday couldn't come soon enough. The bell rings at the end of the day, and with his dance ticket in his back pocket, Cris heads home but quickly changes his mind. He decides to go by one of the only diners in town where Mamá said his dad works. Suddenly, it seems as if someone is driving his vehicle for him. He isn't in control, but it is all fine. It is time. He has waited long enough.

I yell into his ear over and over again, "You can do it, brother! Go over there and talk to him. That's all you have to do."

News travels quickly in a small town, and word has gotten out that Rico is waiting for Cris' visit. People in the town feel sorry for him because he has endured so much loss throughout the years. Our dad lost his brother Carlos at an early age, and now his son, me, who died unexpectedly in a car accident. I wish he would have been closer to us. The guilt of surviving his brother and now his son has to be difficult for him.

You have a chance now, Dad, to make things right with your son. That's all you need to do. I try to communicate with Rico but don't know how much he'll understand.

Cris, I believe, is my best bet. He is busy trying to find Rico.

Cris' plan is to go into the diner and sit down for a cup of coffee or something to see if he can catch a glimpse of Rico. That's all he wants, for now, a simple glimpse. He repeats it in front of his bathroom mirror to practice while I cheer him on. He's wondering if he looks like him? Will Dad be a nice guy? I wonder, too.

Cris

I hop into my pickup, pull out my phone and begin scrolling through my timeline to see if there's anything I need to know. The only thing that interests me right now is the news about the third car. Nope nothing. Someone has to know something about it. I check if there's any local news. *Nada*. Turning to Twitter, I see what's trending. Same ol' stuff. There are some cute dog videos, though. The one where the beagle plays the piano and sings at the same time is one of my favorites. Those always make my day. I also love looking at some of the classic rock videos from the eighties. Pink Floyd tops my list.

Songs always have a way of saying the right thing at exactly the right time. That's why I love music, especially rock. I start the car and drive to the street where the diner is and park right in front. I sit in the truck for a while. I take a deep breath, and then just as Mom taught me, I do the sign of the cross. There is some sort of a calming feeling in reciting the "Hail Mary" over and over. It's a meditation for me, a soothing remedy for my anxiety. Even if I don't have my rosary, I still pray. It doesn't matter.

"You can do this," I tell myself. "I have the power."

I crack open the truck door and quickly shut it. My confidence is gone.

"No, not now. I can't do it. I'm not ready."

Pinching my arm as hard as I can, I turn the engine back on.

I drive home as quickly as I can and park, but do not get out right away. My hand reaches over to the radio dial that reads 109.7. I crank up the volume as loud as it can go. The music penetrates my inner being, my soul. I become one with the sound. It bubbles up in me, the sounds and the waves hit me, vibrating in me. I feel alive from the inside out, from the inner soul to the outer core, alive—alive for once—breathing even as my arm is still throbbing.

Tomorrow is Saturday. It'll be a better day, I reassure myself and get out of the truck. I will have to ask Mom for help. The timing will have to be right.

I head to my room and hurl myself onto the small bed I had neatly made that morning. I turn over to the side table and grab my notebook and pencil. I begin to write my feelings out in the old notebook. It's become my true friend. Only on paper can I share how I truly feel. If I didn't write everything out, I'd surely go crazy.

I remember my teacher telling me I needed to keep a journal and write everything down. At first, I thought she was full of it. Only the nerds do that, not me. Now, I can't be without getting my thoughts down. It's become so normal I've even stopped looking around to make sure no one's looking. I don't care anymore. I'll do it wherever. I continue writing.

I quickly get ready for school and run to the kitchen to fix breakfast before Mom gets up. I grew up helping Mom in the kitchen, not like some guys I know who feel like their moms should serve the men in the family. Grandma always told Mom, "You need to pass on our Mexican traditions to your sons and show them how we respect men." It was hard for her without Dad around. Mamá has had to be the mom and the dad. She's my role model. Besides, I felt that macho stuff is so antiquated.

As I stand at the stove, Mom walks into the kitchen. "¿*M'ijito*, what are you doing up so early?"

"I fixed breakfast for us. *Mira, taquitos*."

On the stove I have a pan with *chorizo con huevos* and on the cast-iron *comal* I have *tortillas* heating up. *Chorizo* with eggs was always Carlos' and my favorite breakfast.

"What's up? Something's going on, I know you, *m'ijo*."

I look away from the stove and into her eyes, defined with dark circles underneath them. They're sunken and swollen with some extra wrinkles.

"Mamá, will you go with me to the diner?"

"What? Why?"

"You know why, Mamá. Please…"

"*M'ijito*, you know how hard this is for me. *No puedo*."

"I need to do this, you need to understand. He's my father, *mi sangre*."

"I understand. I just don't like it. I can understand and not like it, right? You don't know what you're getting yourself into. You go. *Anda*. If you want me to go with you, I'll go. *Yo te espero en el auto*. I'll be there for you if you need me."

I take a deep breath and put my two hands on Mom's shoulders. She looks straight into my eyes. So much needs to be said, but words are not necessary. Mamá kisses me lightly on my cheek and goes to get her purse from her room. She comes back to me, slings the bag over her shoulder and takes a deep breath.

We walk out, leaving the *taquitos de chorizo con huevo* untouched. We get into the pickup, and my stomach is already in knots, with the last thing on my mind being food. I drive straight to the same parking spot I had parked in before. I leave the truck motor running and take off my seat belt.

I focus on Mamá. "You sure you'll be all right?"

"*Sí, m'ijo, no te mortifiques.* I'll be fine here. I'm here if you need me."

"I'll be right back."

I step out of the truck and shut the door. Looking at Mom, I smile and head toward the front door of the diner.

Inside, the diner seems rather empty. It's a sort of combo grocery/diner where all sorts of things are for sale in the front, and there's a pretty cozy restaurant with booths in the back. There aren't many people looking around, drinking coffee or eating burgers, but the smell of fresh-baked bread travels throughout the store, piercing my taste buds and making my mouth water.

In the back is a small kitchen where the cook prepares the food. I have heard that the best chef in town works here, and everyone loves to eat there.

On the large TV screen, you can hear the engines of racing cars rumbling and crowds cheering. There's some sort of stock car race going on, and apparently, people in this town like everything having to do with cars. It seems like a cool store, but I'm not here to look at the merchandise. Well, I am actually here to pretend to look at the merchandise... maybe order a coffee and see what I can figure out. Someone taps my shoulder from behind.

I turn.

"Can I help you, son?"

"Uh, batteries..." I stutter.

"You need batteries?"

"I wanted to see what kind you had."

"Follow me over here."

The man steps out from behind the counter and walks over toward the back of the store, where the batteries are displayed. He is tall and thin with a limp in his walk. His hair is straight, light-brown and a bit on the long side, hitting the edge of his shoulders. He is light-skinned, with a hollow look in his bright, light-brown eyes. When he walks, he keeps one hand in his blue jean pocket and the other holding a big brass ring with lots of keys.

"Are you the one?" I whisper.

"Did you say something?"

"Sorry, I'll have to come back."

"Sure, *m'ijo*. Come back whenever. I'll be here. My name is Rico."

I turn as white as a ghost as I quickly leave the smell of bread, food and plastic behind. The cocktail of aromas is making me nauseous. I want to faint. My heart starts beating unusually fast. Can he see my shirt jumping? My trembling, clammy hands are clearly visible, as if I have seen a piece of myself. It is weirding me out.

I run out of the front door to the pickup and get in. Mom is sitting with her head down in prayer, her rosary wrapped around her hands. The imprint of the beads is embedded in her skin.

"*¡Ay Dios mío! ¿Qué te pasó,* Cris*?*"

"I can't talk about it right now."

Sweating profusely, I start the engine and drive home in silence. When we arrive, I go straight to my bedroom and get under the covers. I grab my arm and pinch it as hard as I can. It will be all right. The dance is coming up, and everything will be all right. I need to rest and try to forget about what happened. As my eyes close, I am calm.

Carlos

Pots and pans are banging loudly in the kitchen. Cris wakes up from his dreams. Mamá is upset. She usually makes extra noise in the kitchen when something is bothering her. This time, Cris knows exactly what that is.

He gets out of bed and heads toward the kitchen. Dragging his feet across the squeaky floor, he covers his ears to shield himself from the clanging.

"Mamá, ¿qué pasa?"

"I'm fine."

"I'm gonna have to see him. You know that. He's my blood, Mamá."

"You don't know the things I do. I've been trying to protect you all these years, but now you're grown up, and I can't stop you."

"Why did you come back here, then? You knew he was here. You knew we'd run into him. You can't run anymore."

"I couldn't do it anymore. It was time to face it and deal with what had to be."

"What is that, Mamá? You can tell me. What did he do?"

"No, I can't. He'll have to tell you himself."

"Fine. I'll go back and talk to him. It'll be fine, don't worry."

Cris reaches out to embrace Mamá as she wipes the tears from her eyes. "I have to go take a shower and get ready for the dance now. You'll be all right?"

"*Sí, m'ijito*, go. I'm fine. You're not like him. You're better. Don't forget that."

"Mamá, I'm not a kid anymore. I can handle the truth."

He goes back to his room, turns on his speaker full blast, pulls out a black shirt and a faded pair of whitewashed blue jeans and lays them on his bed. I go in and sit down on the bed. Cris stops for a moment and looks right at me. He stares right into my eyes as if he wants to talk to me.

Turning around, Cris catches a glimpse of himself in his dresser mirror. Does he look like our dad? Does he have his eyes? Is he like him? Cris then turns sideways to look at his profile and wonders some more, then walks into the shower. A steaming hot shower will do him good right now.

I talk as loud as I can with all of my force. He has to hear me. "You actually have Mom's eyes, but yeah, you do look like him. We both look like him. Well, I think you're more like him."

"Who said that?" Cris jumps out of the shower and spins around, looking in every direction. He runs into the bedroom to see if someone has come in. No one. Only me.

"You heard me? You can hear me, right?"

Cris pivots his head in every direction again and walks up and down in his small bedroom, checking every corner. "Who's here?" He reaches for the volume knob on the stereo and turns it all the way down. "Is someone here?"

"Cris, don't be scared. I'm here to help you. I've always been here with you. It's me, bro."

"Carlos? Weird..." He scrunches his eyes and looks around, then laughs. "Nah...."

He takes his time and begins to relax, wraps a towel around his waist and even starts to sing one of his favorite songs at the top of his lungs. Wow, he can sing!

He steps over to my guitar and picks it up, starts strumming it and continues singing, then laughs and places it back.

"I really have to get dressed now," he says aloud.

He goes to the bathroom mirror and examines his face. No need to shave. He had tried to grow a bit of beard and mustache for the new trending look. It was much easier for him. Yep, it's getting there. Maybe others would think so too. Actually, Dad has a bit of a beard and mustache, too. Interesting.

He quickly gets his clothes thrown on, pulls on his brown cowboy boots and looks at himself in the mirror one last time. The sun has set and the stars are shining outside.

He then reaches into the closet and stares at the letterman jacket hanging as if waiting for him to bring it to life. "You are my connection to my dad and to my brother. I only wish you could talk to me. Please tell me something."

He slips it on and automatically feels a spiritual connection he can't explain. I feel it, too.

"*¡Ay qué chulo!*" Mom can't help but gush as Cris heads for the front door.

"Please, Mamá, I'm no big deal."

"You are more than a big deal, *mi vida*. Look at you, how handsome you are. More importantly, you can see the beauty of your soul in your eyes. Have fun and be safe."

"Don't worry, I'll be fine. Love you, Mamá."

"I love you, *mi amor. Te quiero muchísimo*."

"Mamá, do you ever hear Carlos?"

Mom is startled by the question. "What? Carlos?"

"No, nothing, Mom. I'm just thinking about him, that's all."

"*Qué Dios te bendiga, m'ijito.*" Mamá takes her right hand and makes the sign of the cross on his forehead like she always did for both of us, touching his head, chest and both shoulders.

Cris kisses Mom on the forehead and grabs his keys from where they're hanging on a nail next to a picture of *Santísimo Corazón de Jesús*. He steps out the kitchen door, walks down the wooden steps, heads toward the caliche driveway and gets into his pickup. A dark blanket covers the night, and mist has settled on the front windshield. Cris turns on the truck, then the wipers and, of course, the radio full blast.

"Yes! I love this," he tells himself as he starts singing and moving to "Spirit In The Sky" by Norman Greenbaum.

As the song comes to an end, Cris finds himself passing in front of the diner. He sees a figure inside, even though the lights are off. The lights flicker. He slows down.

"He must be working late. Good for him."

After peering into the front window, Cris drives away.

Cris

My head is buzzing, and my hair is blowing as the wind crashes against my face. I love driving with the window rolled down. The radio is cranked up and the seats of my truck are dancing with Bon Jovi's "It's My Life."

The high school is only a few blocks from downtown. It's a typical, traditional high school with a big M in the front for Malton and a football field to the side. During football season, the entire town goes out to the games to support the team. That's the highlight of the week in a small town. Football brings everyone together. It had bonded my brother and me in a weird way. I didn't like football, but I supported him. I was his number one fan.

As I approach, I notice the parking lot is actually full. That's a good sign. The school is old and outdated like the ones you see in the movies from the 1950s. It's the same school our parents went to years ago and probably their parents too. They most likely sat in the exact same desks I sit in too.

"They must have had their dances here, too. Now that's totally weird," I say aloud.

After I park my pickup, I sit for a bit. I don't like to rush into anything. I take time to think about what's about to happen. The evening is a bit cold, the moon is about to burst through the clouds, and some stars are scattered. It's as if someone had just taped them up to the sky and they could be taken down at any time. It looks like a picture someone has painted for an art gallery.

I reach into my back pocket to make sure the ticket's in my wallet. I open it, and right next to my twenty-dollar bill is the black ticket. I'm about to get out when...

"*Bang!*" A hand hits the driver's side window, then another hand is banging even louder on the door. I flinch and look out to see who it is. My heart is racing as Damian pops up and starts laughing.

"What's the matter with you? You scared me, *pendejo!*" I yell at him.

"Got ya, *vato*, made you jump! You coming in or what?"

"Yeah, I'm coming."

I step out of the pickup and walk through the parking lot with Damian. He's wearing a western-style shirt, jeans and boots.

"You should have seen your face!"

"Yeah, yeah, yeah."

"So, are you ready to have fun?"

"I guess."

"Hey, you can take your jacket off now. It's not even that cold."

"Naw, I'm keeping it."

"It's so old school, dude."

"Yep, I'm keeping it on. I don't know about you, but I like old school. It's comfortable for me."

"Whatever, I'll check you later. I gotta go. I'm supposed to work at the snack bar but I'm gonna try to get out of it."

"Are you going to meet with the girl?" he adds.

"Yes, that's the plan," I say and Damian walks away.

I walk around the gym to get a feel of the night. The music and lights penetrate the walls, making them vibrate. The dance floor is starting to get packed with teens jumping and dancing some strange moves.

I find a corner to settle into and sense someone come stand right next to me. I inhale a sweet mixture of flowers and herbal tea.

"They dance a little different here, don't they?" Selena says.

I smile at her, "You're obviously new here, right?"

Smiling back, "No, not really."

"Wow, so what can you tell me about this place," I ask.

"Well, most everyone from here has been here a long time. Everyone knows everyone. And not everyone is who they appear to be."

I tilt my head, "That's a coincidence. I mean, it's kinda weird. Selena, right?"

She peers up at me. "So, you took a break from your reading tonight, Cris?"

"Yep, I needed a break." I step a bit closer so I don't have to yell and I slide my hands into the deep pockets of my jacket.

"Me too," she says in a soft voice I can barely hear.

"A break from what?"

"Well, I guess you can say I've been in training. I have a new hobby."

"What did you say? I can barely hear you."

The dance music shifts from upbeat to soft, slow music as if on cue. How can anyone resist the sound of Cyndi Lauper's "Time After Time."

Without thinking, I grab Selena's hand and walk onto the dance floor, swaying and singing in harmony.

"I love this song," I say.

Spinning and floating, Selena blurts out, "No, *I* love this song. It's my favorite. The line, 'You will find me'… it's beyond magical."

As I lift her up in my arms, she's weightless. Is she for real? "My parents used to listen to this. Isn't that hard to believe?"

"I know, how weird. My mom loved it too, and that was like a million years ago."

I stare into her bewitching eyes. "My parents used to be so in love with each other. They met right here in this same high school. Now, they can't stand each other. They separated and my dad doesn't even know I'm alive. I don't even know why I'm telling you all this."

"I know how you feel. I don't even have a dad," Selena says. "And my mom and her friend also don't seem to know I'm alive either. Sometimes I want to get so far away from them, so they'll understand how I really feel. But then I think, 'No, no, no. I definitely can't. They'll miss me if I leave them.' You know?"

I nod my head in agreement. "Yeah, I get it. Except, I really do have a dad. He just doesn't know me or he doesn't care to know me. At all! He left when I was tiny and hasn't bothered to visit. Well, my mom didn't want him to. That's why he never did. Still, you'd think he would have at least tried to see me. I've spent most of my life hoping and praying and nothing. You know how that makes me feel?"

Selena spins a few times and looks right into my eyes. "I don't get what your dad is thinking. He must have a reason. I can guess, though…. I've run away from home before."

"You did? Why?"

"I don't know… My heart wanted to get away for a while. I needed to explore… you know?" She says, brushing her hair back off her shoulders.

"Yeah, I get you. So, how old were you when you ran away?"

Selena places her hands on her curly brown hair and brushes it all the way down to her sides, lifting the edges of her short skirt and looking down at it. "About this old, fifteen. Actually, it was a few months ago and not the first time. It's just that my mom treats me like a kid sometimes. I just want her to treat me like me, Selena. I have to keep reminding her that I'm not Lilly, like she always calls me. She named me after her. Her name is Lillith, and I hate it. That's why I go by my middle name." She laughs.

She looks different without her glasses. I guess she's wearing contacts tonight and I can't stop looking at her.

"My mom went ballistic when I ran away. It was like an explosion of the worst kind. You know, I don't blame her, I guess. I've always been a sort of rebel." She smiles.

I mutter, "Without a cause?"

Swinging in rhythm, she answers, "Those are the best kind. After the incident, I gave her a heart locket with an owl engraving and promised her I'd never leave her. I felt horrible for putting her through that. I'm not a terrible daughter, you know. She was so happy. Now she's super nice to me all the time."

I look down and notice she's wearing a gold chain with a locket. "Where'd you get that locket?"

"Oh, an old friend gave it to me when we were kids. My mom always loved mine, that's why I got her a matching one."

I tilt my head back and narrow my eyes. "Why an owl?"

Selena half smiles. "Oh, she just likes owls. That's all. You know what they say about owls in our culture."

I take her hand and walk her off the dance floor as the music continues to play softly. In the background one couple seems to be having a great time, laughing and singing together and then in a split second storming out in tears. "Come on, babe. Give me a chance," I overhear the guy say.

On the other end of the dance floor, the cool kids are dancing with each other, pretending to be on some YouTube video.

"How can they all seem so perfect?" I ask.

"They're just like us. Don't ever think any of them are any better than you are. They are not perfect."

I take a deep breath. "They just seem like they have it all together. Their parents are probably together. They probably have a nice family. You know, their dad loves them. Not like me. I have none of that."

"Forget about it, Cris! Let's have fun."

"You're right. We're going to have the best night."

Selena looks up at me and smiles. I notice her long curly dark lashes accenting her eyes. Stepping up on her toes, she wraps her arms around me and kisses me lightly on the cheek. I hadn't felt that way as long as I can remember. It's an instant connection, as if we're meant to be together. We seem to understand each other like no one in the world can.

"Let's get out of here. It's getting stuffy. I need some air. I need to breathe," I say.

Damian comes up from behind and grabs my shoulder. "Hey, *vato*! Where ya going?"

"Hey, this is Selena. Sorry, friend, but we gotta get going."

"The night is young. Come hang out with us. We're gonna go out for a drive."

"Raincheck... I have to get Selena home soon. Check ya later."

"See ya on Monday."

As we walk out the double doors and into the parking lot, a gust of freezing air hits us, and raindrops start pouring down on us.

Selena giggles, "I didn't know it was going to be this cold or that it was going to rain, did you?"

I take off my letterman jacket and wrap it around Selena's shoulders. "No, but here, put this on."

I put my arm around her, and we run toward the pickup, splashing in the puddles beginning to form in the parking lot.

"Thanks, Cris. I was freezing."

The rain continues to pour in gusts as we settle into the truck.

"Maybe we should let the rain die down a bit," Selena says. I turn on the engine.

"We'll be fine, don't worry."

I turn on the radio to my favorite rock music and start to head out of the high school parking lot.

Carlos

The wind is fierce, and the blades of grass have wilted crowns. Whirling in the mystical mist are the tiny bugs dancing around the light posts outside of our house.

Mom is sitting in our small frame home watching her favorite *novela*, hoping Cris will get back early. Of course, she wants him to have fun and dance, but something is bothering her. I nestle up close to her and try to rest my head on her shoulders, but no matter how hard I try, I can't do it. She looks up and smiles briefly. I know she is thinking about me.

Wrapping her hands is a brown wooden rosary, she softly rubs bead by bead between her thumb and index finger. She has grown accustomed to reciting the rosary prayers repeatedly throughout the day to ease her worries and send special prayers for her sons.

Sitting on her worn-out sofa, she keeps peering out the window to see if any car headlights can be seen. It's still outside, quiet. Nothing.

"*Ay, Dios mío, cuida a m'ijito. Es tan inocente. Santa María Madre de Dios...*" she continues with her prayers.

She will not sleep until Cris comes home. Tonight, it is going to be a late night. The soap opera and late-night news just ended with the same old depressing stories. Now, Mamá is watching a movie. During the week, she watches Jimmy Kimmel because she loves watching Guillermo, but usually falls asleep halfway through.

"*Qué mortificaciones,*" she mutters and begins a *Padre nuestro*... Over and over, bead by bead, she chants Hail Marys and Our Fathers until the rosary slips through her tired fingers and into her lap. Her head falls to the pillow on the edge of the sofa.

Cris

On the other side of our small town, Selena and I sit in the pickup, talking as if we've known each other our entire lives. We laugh and talk like we have forever to do it. There is no sense of time, no thought of calling home, no worries at all. The rain has subsided, and the smell of freshness is in the air.

"I've never been happier than I am right now. I don't want tonight to ever end," I confess.

"Cris, it doesn't have to end. It can go on. You have to believe that."

"I do. I believe that."

"Promise me then no matter what, you will always be with me."

"What do you mean? Why are you saying that? Of course, I will. You're the best thing that ever happened to me. You made me realize I don't even need my dad anymore. It's his loss, not mine. You're what matters to me. If I meet him, fine. If not, I'll be fine. What matters is I've found you."

"No, Cris, you're what matters. Remember that."

"Yes, I matter. But more importantly, we matter."

As we peer out the pickup window, the golden sun crests and blends into the clouds. Time has paused for us.

"Look at the sun. It's beautiful! It's golden! What's that poem 'Nothing Gold Can Stay' that talks about staying golden? Did you ever read it? Who's the poet?"

"Robert Frost."

"Yeah, I love it. I used to know it by heart." She looks at her watch. "I have to get home. I don't want to, but my mom will be so upset. We better go."

"I'm sorry, I didn't mean to keep you out this late."

"No… it's my mom. She won't understand."

We embrace one last time, and I turn on the ignition and put the truck in drive. Selena rests her head on my shoulder. Without touching any dials, the music comes to life in my truck.

"My radio's been acting wacko. I need to get it checked out."

"Good taste," she says.

I look at her, and she winks at me as the radio plays "*Amor Prohibido*" by Selena.

I turn up the volume. "Yeah, that was my parents' favorite song. It's strange that it's playing on that station." The radio cuts off in mid song.

"Well, all right…. Where do you live?"

"I live super close to here. You can turn up ahead."

"Cassandra used to live around here," I tell her. "She was my brother's girlfriend, but she moved away. I know this area."

I drive and every few minutes glance at Selena and smile.

"Here, turn here. It's that white house. But you can leave me here so I can walk."

"No, I'm not letting you walk."

"Really, I don't want to make any noise. If I wake up my mom, she'll freak out. I'll have to sneak in."

"Are you sure? Let me walk you to the door. I can't leave you here on the side of the road."

Selena leans over and kisses me.

"No, please. I have to do it this way. You don't know my mom. I'm doing us both a favor, believe me. You may hear things about me. Please remember us tonight. I'll see you soon."

Biting my bottom lip and shaking my head, I try to stop her. "Hear things? What things?"

She waves at me and blows me a kiss. "Nothing."

I watch Selena walk to her house with the winding sidewalk and take a deep breath.

I begin to drive back home, still in a dreamlike state. The radio turns on and Selena continues singing her song.

"Did this really happen?"

Carlos

My brother is dropping Selena off, and I have to stick close to her to find out what she's up to. She seems nervous. I can tell because she keeps wiping the sweat from her forehead when Cris isn't looking. Maybe she can sense me.

When she saw him at school, I noticed how she was instantly drawn to him. Yeah, my brother stands out. He's different from the rest of the cookie-cutter kids. I guess she felt something real about him. Out of everyone bumping into her in the hall that day, he was the one who helped her. No one seemed to care. I guess it was her lucky day. But why? I saw her toss her amulet into her purse. Now, here we are.

Selena knew something was up with the Selena song. Cris didn't get it. He thinks it's his pickup, but this girl figured it out. Music is my thing. That's the easiest way for me to break through.

She gets out of the pickup and starts walking up the sidewalk. Sure enough, her mom is waiting for her inside, holding onto her cigarette, puffing her nerves away.

"Where were you, young lady?" she says in an aggressive tone.

Selena pretends her mother's not there and heads for the stairs.

"Don't you go up there. I'm talking to you."

Ms. Cano grabs her arm, and Selena turns around and gives her an evil look.

"What? I didn't do anything," Selena says as she opens up her purse and searches for something.

"Who were you with?"

"It doesn't matter. You're not going to let me see him anymore, right?"

"Who was it? I need to know," her mother insists.

"You don't know him. He's a good person... a decent person.... But what do you care? I'm happy, Mom. Don't you want that for me?"

"I asked you... who were you with?"

"Fine. I was with... Cris." Selena smiles and closes her eyes.

Her mom turns as white as a ghost and puts her hand over her forehead. She reaches for the phone on the coffee table by the sofa and begins dialing.

"Who are you calling?"

"You little... you're doing this to me on purpose aren't you? Jack, Lilly needs help. She just got home... out all night. I know... with that boy, Cris."

"Mom! Stop! Why are you doing this? What does he care?"

"Just walked in now. He dropped her off. The whole night out! How dare she. Yes, I understand. I'll try."

Her mother slams the phone down and looks back at Selena, crushing her cigarette down in the ashtray and splattering ashes all over the place.

I hate those cancer sticks. They stink, but she doesn't seem to care. Poor Selena has to live with this mom, and the smoke enveloping the room makes it worse. Selena coughs and takes a deep breath.

"Why do you keep doing... Don't you remember when I had my asthma attack? You had to take me to the hospital in the middle of the night because of your stupid cigarettes. The doctor told you to stop," Selena yells.

"This isn't about me, Selena. You always change things around, don't you?"

Selena glares, reaches into her purse and rubs something between her fingers. "You really shouldn't do that. It's bad for your health. Something might happen to you. Why'd you call him? What's he gonna do?"

Selena steps down from the stairs and sits down on the sofa. "I know Sheriff Tanner's on his way over here, right? That's why he's been overprotective? Well, I don't know why I have to listen to him or why you listen to him."

"Look, Lilly," her mother says, now sobbing, "I don't want anything to happen to you. You're all I have. Jack can help us because of his position. He needs to approve of this boy. He knows everyone and their backgrounds. I'm trying to help you. You understand, don't you? Jack is our friend."

"I'm not Lilly, I've told you. My name is Selena. No one calls me Lilly except you. Are you crazy, Mom?" Selena says, shaking her head at her mom and breathing heavily. "We're in high school, and I really like him. Why do you have to ruin everything for me all the time."

"Stop, Lilly!"

Selena grabs a pillow from the sofa and throws it across the room. The lights in the living room start blinking on and off. "No, you stop! You're a life ruiner! That's what you and Sheriff Tanner are. You're both life ruiners!"

Standing menacingly with one hand on her hip and pointing at her daughter, Ms. Cano threatens, "If you want to stay in school, you'll listen to me. If not, I'll pull you out again and homeschool you. I don't trust anyone. It's for your own protection."

Now it's Selena's turn to reach for the phone. "And you wonder why I run away," Selena blurts out and gets her phone from her purse. "Rico is the only one who understands me. He's a real friend. He'll listen to me."

"Yes, call Dad," I try to say, getting close to her, whispering in ear.

"Rico cannot help us," her mother counters. "He has other issues to deal with. His entire family is in trouble. Stay away from them."

"What the hell, lady. Please don't say we're in trouble when you're here yelling at your daughter," I say to her in vain. "I may be dead, but I'll do what I can to help my family, and your daughter is going to help me."

"Uggghhh!!!!" Selena slams the phone down on the sofa.

The sound of a truck pulls up in the driveway, and heavy footsteps make their way to the front door. They know that sound. The mom rushes to open the two deadbolts on the door and lets Sheriff Tanner in. He comes into the living room where Selena is sitting, grabs a chair and flips it backwards to sit on. The room is dim, stuffy and still smells of smoke. He looks at Selena and starts to tell her about the accident. He acts like she doesn't know about it. Ms. Cano lights another cigarette.

Jack Tanner is attempting to mouth words of wisdom: "You may not understand all of this, but the terrible accident that happened a few months ago was caused by the driver of a pickup truck. I know who the driver is and I'm going to bring him in for questioning. They're not going to get away with my son's death. I'll make sure he pays." His eyes are small lines under his thick eyebrows. They move up and down as he talks.

Selena's mom sits quietly on the sofa, nodding in agreement and puffing away.

"What's the matter with both of you? Everyone knows it was an accident," Selena says.

"Nooo! It was not an accident. I'll prove it, and they will pay. Rico and his son will pay," the sheriff says, pounding his fist.

"Rico? He wouldn't hurt a fly. He would never do that. I don't believe you. And who is his son, anyway?" Selena yells.

"You don't know? Cris is about to get into some deep trouble," he says.

"Cris? My Cris?"

"That's right. And, if you know what's good for you, you'll stay away from him, or you'll be in trouble, too. I'm not messing around. I'm serious."

I feel like an alien. I'm suddenly alone on an unknown planet, and no one can come save me. I need an extra life or at least a boost.

Selena gets right up into the sheriff's space. "You can't make me do anything. I can see him if I want to. You think because you carry a gun and have some stupid badge, I have to listen to you. I don't!"

With that, Sheriff Tanner laughs. "You go ahead. Do what you want," he says. "I promise he'll end up in jail faster than you can flip your hair back."

"I don't care if you and Mom are special friends or whatever the hell you are. You can't make me do anything and you can't arrest him. You need proof."

"That we have, young lady. Just you wait and see."

Selena let's out a loud scream, "Uggggghhhh!!! What the heck is happening? I don't want anyone to go to jail."

Her mom sits back and smiles.

"FINE!!!!" Selena yells, making both Jack and her mother cover their ears. Then, she runs upstairs and throws herself on her unmade bed surrounded by band posters: Korn, Nirvana, Panic at the Disco.

Think, think, think Selena... She reaches for a strange-looking reference book with symbols on her desk. She opens it while dialing Angélica, her friend, the one who has guided her through her craft.

"Ang, you're my mentor and the only one who understands me. I need help. Hey... he was here," she says in tears. "He told me to stay away from Cris or he'll arrest him. Why is he doing this?" Her breathing is fast, and her phone is getting slippery. She tries to keep the conversation quiet, so she goes into the bathroom and locks the door. Reaching for tissues, she wipes away tears, opens the medicine cabinet and looks through the various herbs she has stocked up there. "There has to be a spell I can use to stop this madness, Ang."

"Selena, listen to him. He's serious. Cris is in some trouble, and I don't want you getting hurt. Don't go against the sheriff right now. I'll talk to you about it later. I can sense these things."

Selena hangs up and closes the medicine cabinet. Suddenly, in the mirror, she notices a shadow.

"Who's there?" She turns around and doesn't see me.

Again, she opens the cabinet and closes it, but nothing. There's nothing there.

Selena gets out of the small bathroom and lies down on her bed again, pulls the covers completely over her head with her clothes and shoes on and continues crying. "Why can't I have a normal life. Just when I start to feel like everything is falling into place, they take everything away from me. I have to find out what's going on. I'm not going to let them control me like this. I have to find out what they know about the accident."

I try to mess with the lights, switching them on and off. It's a simple trick. "I can help," I say, trying to be heard again.

"Who said that?" She yanks the covers off, jumps out of bed and checks her phone to see if she left it on. Nothing. It's off. "Is someone in here?"

"So, you can hear me? Can you see me, too? I knew you'd be able to." I'm making progress.

She grabs her phone to call. It's dead. "Who the heck is this? Where are you? What the…? I know my phone was on and charged," she says, spinning in circles, looking in all directions.

"Don't be scared.… I'm not here to hurt you. I need your help," I say.

She runs back into the bathroom and slams the door and leans her back on it. "Leave me alone!"

I think I can hear her heart beating, and I definitely see goosebumps pop up on her arms. She knows I'm here. I focus with all my might, and my energy appears right in front of her. I'm like a magnet. I can't control it. She has a power drawing me in. She finally sees me, but doesn't freak out. She's probably seen others like me before.

"What the hell do you want?" she blurts out.

"You know Cris." I have her attention.

"How do you know him?" she asks.

"He's my brother."

"And who the hell are you?"

"Carlos. Listen, please. There's information you need to know about. I found it out by hanging out with Big J. It'll help you, but you have to get to the auto shop at the edge of town… now."

"What? What do you mean information? Hello???"

"I can't say anymore."

"What happened? Carlos? You gone?"

My energy is used up. It takes everything out of me to communicate. I'm new at this, and what I have learned is that any little thing you do to try to get someone's attention, like switching lights on and off or moving objects, depletes you. You have to recharge. At least, I have to until I get better at this dead thing.

Selena jumps back into bed, covers herself with the blanket and sinks in. "What just happened? I wasn't dreaming. I know I can do some things, but..."

The tears soak her pillow, and she flips it over. I know she's thinking about Cris. I picture them together, dancing and laughing with each other. That's what I want for my brother, for him to have a happy life. I need to do something good for him while I can, so I can move on. I can't stay here forever. Specially with Big J hanging around, no thanks, I don't want him with me forever in the afterlife. I need to see what I can do to get me to my next level.

"What's he going to think now? What am I going to tell him? I can't let them arrest him."

Still sobbing, Selena reaches under the bed and grabs a small suitcase. She opens it, and there are some strange things in there I've never seen before and some medicine-like containers with funny-looking labels. She grabs them and sticks them into her backpack. When Selena hears her mom get in the shower, she leaves. She checks her phone. It's working, fully charged.

Cris sneaks in past Mom, who is fast asleep on the sofa. The TV has automatically turned off. Sleep mode. He leans into her and almost nudges her shoulders, then backs off. He decides not to wake her. I know he must be dying to talk to her about his night. I can see it in his eyes. He floats into his room and plops himself onto his small bed with his clothes and shoes still on. With sleep overcoming him, he drifts off with the biggest smile painted on his face and the scent of love still lingering.

―――

"*M'ijito*, when did you come in? I must have dozed off. *Te estuve esperando*," Mamá says, waking up Cris in the morning.

Cris rolls over and looks up at Mom, stretching out his arms to hug her. "Mamá. *Tanto que te quiero*."

"*¿Qué tienes, m'ijo? Te miras* a little weird. You okay?"

"Mom, I met a girl. She is the best thing that's ever happened to me."

"Cris… be careful. Things don't always seem as perfect as they are. Slowly, *m'ijito*. Take your time."

"No, Mom. I know. I can feel it in my heart. We danced all night. Then we ended up talking into the morning. I even lent her Carlos' jacket."

"You what??? Lent her your dad's jacket? How could you? That jacket meant everything to your dad and to Carlos too, you know that. *¿Qué te pasa, m'ijo?*"

"Oh, no! I forgot to get the jacket back. Sorry, Mom."

"Sorry? No. That's not good enough."

"Well, I guess it's a perfect excuse to see her again. I'll go over to her house later. Mom, don't worry about me. I'm so happy! Please be happy for me."

"If you say so, *m'ijito*. I have a bad feeling about this, *no sé*, but go take a shower and get dressed. I'll fix you breakfast. *¿Quieres huevo con chorizo?*" she says, heading to the kitchen, shaking her head in disapproval and mumbling to herself.

Then she grabs her cell phone and makes a call. "He met a girl," she whispers into the phone.

"*¿Quién es?*" the voice says.

"*No sé.* He didn't tell me her name. I know..."

"Distract him. Don't let him get hurt. We can't let it happen again," the voice says with a warning.

"I'll try." She quickly takes the Chorizo de San Manuel brand sausage out of the refrigerator, as well as the carton of eggs and the *tortillas de harina* she made from scratch yesterday. That was our favorite breakfast. She used to tell us it was also our dad's favorite breakfast. Funny how we were so similar.

The smell of the spices permeates the kitchen and the small house. *Chorizo* has a way of teasing the nose and the taste buds, which brings Cris into the kitchen.

"Smells great, Mom. I'm starving."

"*Listo, m'ijito.* It's ready. Sit down," she says.

Cris pours himself a cup of coffee and places it on the small Formica table, then grabs a plate and slaps a *tortilla de harina* on it, loading it with his favorite *chorizo con huevo*. Mamá does the same, and they sit down together and say a quick prayer before eating.

Oh, how I remember eating this food. Now, I don't even get hungry. It's nice being close to it and enjoying the memories of how the hot spices tingled in my mouth. I don't know how long it's been since I ate. It's so weird. Sitting with them, going through the motions.

"So, tell me, Cris..."

He takes a huge bite from his taco, then sips his hot black coffee. "Mamá, I think I'm in love."

"You can't be in love, *m'ijo.* How can you be in love? You don't even know this girl."

"I feel as if I've always known her. It's as if we've been part of each other for eternity."

"*M'ijo*, I'm your mom, and you are the most important person to me in the world. I won't let you get hurt. It's my job to protect you. You know that, right?"

"You don't need to protect me, Mom. You need to take care of yourself. I'm fine."

Before Cris can finish his taco, he stands up and grabs his head, feeling faint. He shakes it off, then picks up his plate and cup, washes them in the sink and puts them away in the cabinet. Since he was a small kid, he has picked up after himself and not depended on Mamá to do everything for him.

"Are you alright, *m'ijo*?"

"I'm feeling a bit strange. I'm not sure."

"*Ay, m'ijito*, we need to take care of it before it gets worse. You know how *delicad*o you are, especially about things like this… love. You can't mess around too much with strong emotions."

Mamá always reminds Cris of when he first experienced the *mal de ojo,* the evil eye someone had cast on him, and how hard it was to cure him.

"Mom, please… It's not *ojo*."

"*M'ijito*, it was not too long ago when I had to call your grandmother to break that spell when you got sick, remember?"

"But, Mom! It was a stomach flu. I got something at school."

"No, I took you to the doctor, and it wasn't no stomach flu, *m'ijo*. It was when we were living here, and you all were in elementary school. Don't try to forget. You know you got better when Grandma came and worked her special powers on you. And, I ended up taking you both back to Houston with the *familia* because someone was trying to hurt you. I had to protect you."

Yeah, someone was trying to hurt both of us at school. It was that mean bully, Big J. He hated us, and I don't even know why. Cris was the smartest kid in class. He didn't even have to study, he simply knew everything, maybe that's why.

Mamá took him to Dr. García, but he couldn't find anything wrong with Cris. It was Grandma who came with her eggs and *lo curó del mal de ojo*. She knew how to do all that weird stuff. With a glass of water in one hand and a raw egg in the other, she worked her magic. The ritual would begin with rubbing an egg on his stomach and after praying and chanting for who knows how long, she cracked the white shell, poured out the gooey white yolk into a glass of water and she read the egg to see if he was cured. It worked. She did it one time to me, too. We felt better but hated the egg thing.

"Fine, I remember. I did feel better," Cris confesses, "but Grandma always makes me feel better when she comes. You don't have to protect me anymore, Mom. I can protect myself and my family."

"Well, if it's not *ojo*, maybe it's something else. Your grandmother can cure you."

"No, Mom, I don't need to be cured this time."

With that, Cris kisses her on the forehead and heads to our room.

I sit with Mamá and try to hold her hand.

The days are a blur. Wow! My *primos* are here, and I haven't seen them in forever. I love my *primos*. Too bad it took my funeral to get us all together. They came from Houston and are sticking around maybe a bit longer. Aunts, uncles, cousins, non-relatives and all types of people are all coming and going at our house.

"*¡Ven a comer, m'ijo!*" The *tías* call Cris after heating up some homemade *carne guisada*, rice and beans with fresh flour *tortillas*. He's getting the royal treatment. It will not surprise me if I see a red carpet somewhere. I can't smell, but I bet the spices are kicking. They're bringing food, sitting on our porch and hanging around outside the house with ice chests. We never had so much food in our home before, and now that we do, I can't even eat it. They've even brought some homemade *tamales*, my favorite. I guess I'll follow everyone around and just watch these people eat and enjoy.

The *tías* from Houston take over the kitchen and start heating up the big pot of menudo they made the night before. They cut up onions, cilantro, peppers and lemons to serve with their masterpiece. I peek into the pot. I used to love this delicacy, complete with pig's feet. Grandma always said, "*No es menudo si no usas patas de marrano.*" I repeat it to myself. One of my aunts looks over her shoulder as if she senses me.

"*Tía,* it's me, I'm here."

Nothing. She goes back to her kitchen duties.

The ladies from church are here praying with Mamá and making her hot *manzanilla* tea for her nerves. Grandma gives her special remedies and prays over her. The church ladies go into our kitchen like it's their own and start heating up rice, beans and *carne guisada*. It's weird to see some people I don't even know at the house. Some of them start sweeping, some wash dishes, some clean the bathroom. They all want to help. It's just too weird. They're even going into our bedroom and sitting on my bed. Hey... that's my bed. The only one not there is our dad.

The men hang out in the front yard, drinking beer and huddling as if listening to a football game on TV. Some kids run around chasing each other. They have a fancy barbeque pit set up that one of my *tíos* brought in the back of his pickup, and they're cooking some *fajitas* and sausage. Man, they really know how to throw a pre-funeral party.

It's a strange feeling. As hard as I try to talk to anyone, no one can hear me.

"Hey! Hey! Hey!" I yell right in their faces. I stomp around the house and even chase the kids outside, but nothing. I think one of my little cousins sees me. I go up to him, he stops running and stares right at me. He's not freaking out. Then they call him to go inside. He runs in, and I follow.

"Hi, *primito*... Can you see me?"

He grabs onto his mom's leg.

"It's all right, no need to be scared. I'm your cousin."

"Carlos," he says.

His mom looks down at him. "*Ay, m'ijito*. We all miss him."

"Carlos is here, Mommy."

"*M'ijito*, Carlos will always be with us."

He runs back outside and plays with his other cousins. So cool.

Mamá had to go to the funeral home today to take the funeral director, Mr. Luna, some clothes for me. She was going to take my letterman jacket, but Cris stopped her. He took the jacket from her and held it close to his chest.

"No, Mamá, please. Let me take it.... I want to drape it over his coffin. It's something I want to do for him."

"Fine, *m'ijo*, if that's how you feel." She takes it from him and puts the jacket back in the closet.

Tomorrow—they say they're going to have my funeral. That's going to be weird. *My funeral*. I hate funerals. I've always hated them. Some people hate funerals, but me, well you would never catch me at one. That's for sure. I never go with Mom when she asks me to. Who wants to see someone in a wooden box all dressed up and stiff? When Cris and I were about six, our grandfather passed away. I loved him. He was a truck driver, and one night he didn't come home from his trip. Grandma was devastated when she got a call from his boss telling her of my grandfather's heart attack while unloading his shipment. Mom was crushed, and she wanted us to go see him at the same Luna's Funeral Home my body's at now.

Mom prepared us so we wouldn't be scared when we saw Grandpa stiff and cold on display. "He's going to be dressed up and he'll be in a coffin... it's like a wooden box."

"Why a box? Is it like a basket? Will he be wearing his jeans and boots like he always does?" I asked.

"Grandma wants him to look his best when we say goodbye to him."

As we arrived at the building, there were men standing outside in circles, smoking and talking. We cut through them and entered the home where Grandpa was and were greeted by a lady wearing a black suit. Mamá took us to the room where my grandfather was on display, but I didn't want to go in.

"No, I don't want to see him in a basket. I don't want to see him dressed up and cold," I insisted, crying like the six-year-old I was. I ran out of the crowded room filled with grownups crying and my grandmother screaming shrilly,"*Mi amor, mi vida, ¿por qué?*"

Mamá came after me. "*M'ijito*, it's all right. You don't have to see him if you don't want to. You saw him all the time. He knows that."

The lady in the black suit came up to Mom and me, offering a box of tissues. "Don't worry, I'll take him into the lounge where we have *pan dulce* and hot chocolate. He can wait for you there. Some of his other relatives will be there."

"Is that all right, *m'ijito*?"

I nod and go with the lady, attracted by the sweet bread and chocolate.

After that experience, I never wanted to go back to anyone's funeral. I had dreams of Grandpa getting out of his wooden box, wearing his fancy suit and telling me he was all right for years. I don't want to see anyone in a casket. It freaks me out. They say it's something everyone has to do in order to have closure and say goodbye. I don't want to say goodbye. I'm still here. I know some people must be able to hear or see me. For sure, the little girl at the hospital saw me. I'll have to find her. She can talk to me. As for tomorrow, I guess I'll go check it out. I mean, it is for me, right?

Mamá's dressed in her black, funeral dress. Her eyes are so swollen from crying all night, you can hardly see her eyelashes. She and Cris are on their way to the funeral home so they can see me before everyone else gets there. I heard the *tías* say they were helping Mom by chipping in to pay for it all. I'm glad. That's what families do. Mom doesn't have any money.

There's soft music playing, and the pews are lined up like in our old church. In the front is the wooden box on display, as if I were the main character in a play. I'm the center of attention, surrounded by candles and flowers. Weird.

I don't know if I want to see my body there. I hate it. I never liked much attention. Maybe I won't look. I know, I'll go but stay in the back and watch from there. That way, I can leave if I want to. I guess it's a way to say goodbye for now because it's not a definite goodbye. It's not like we leave forever. Look at me, I'm here. We are always with our loved ones. Some of us have to figure out how to communicate with others because we're in a different form—sort of like shapeshifters.

I stay in the back when Mom and Cris go to the seats in the front. Cassandra doesn't want to go up to it. She waits. It's hard for her. Besides, she and Damian were recently released from the hospital. She sits close to the front with Damian and doesn't even pick up her head. She's tough. I know she'll be fine.

I have to admit, I'm curious. Is my body really in there? How do I look? Good, I hope. I decide to approach and take a peek. Jesus Christ Almighty, the image sends shivers down my spine. I thrust myself all the way to the back of the room. That cannot be me. No way. No freaking way. I'm shaking, and my heart is beating uncontrollably, if I still have one. I'm not sure anymore. Why did they open that box? The body in there does not look like me. Maybe the clothes, but I look puffy and rubbery. They put makeup on me. No wonder I didn't want to see myself. Forget it. I focus on the family. I try to get my relatives attention. Maybe there's been a mistake. Maybe I'm living a nightmare. No one sees me.

In the back of the gloomy room, I recognize the little girl from the hospital. She's sitting with her parents. It's that man. He's the mean one. The sheriff. I don't know why they're here. She keeps turning around to look at me. I know she can see me. I get up next to her and look right at her.

"Can you see me?" I ask her.

She nods yes.

"Are you scared?" I smile at her.

She shakes her head, no. She has two pigtails with small bows in them that bounce when she moves.

Trying to smile, I talk to her, "I'm here to help. I'm an angel." She just stares at me, so I continue, "Most people can't see me. I wish my family had the same powers as you do. Can you see others?"

Again, she nods, yes.

"Do they scare you?"

She looks right at me and whispers to me. "No, I only see the nice ones."

"Can you see your brother?"

"No. I'm trying," she says.

"I'm so happy you can see me and talk to me. You give me hope. I'll talk to you later."

"Promise?"

"Promise."

Her dad asks her if she's all right. She nods, yes, and waves goodbye to me.

The next day is Big J's funeral. His family is having his funeral on the same day as some other deceased person since they have two chapels. It's like a combo or something. I'm glad mine was first. I like getting things out of the way. At least Mamá is done with that part. I guess that's why Big J's family went by, to get an idea of what to expect. I decide to hang around and wander over to Big J's area. Everything looks the same, but this time it's Big J's body that's in the wooden box on display. There are tons of people in the lobby area. Big J's dad knows everyone.

I don't want to see either one of them, so I stay toward the back and watch the people come and go. Big J's poor mother is heartbroken. I feel bad for her. She's cradling a box of tissues, blotting her wet, red eyes with a soaked one.

"I feel bad for her too, you know," a familiar voice says.

I turn around, and there he is, a spirit kid hanging around the back of the room with me.

He's the same one I thought I'd seen at the hospital and in my room. He's much clearer now. The same tight shirt.

The voice again comes out of nowhere. "Hey, you, Carlos? Follow me."

I focus, and then right before me, he appears. My nemesis. Super clear.

"I know we weren't friends before… Well, I guess I was downright mean to you. But I sort of need your help now. I haven't figured out how to talk to anyone else who can see or hear me. You can see me, right?"

I pull away from him, "Look, man, I don't have time for you. I never did, and I certainly don't now. Get away from me! You were a hateful, racist bully."

He's fading in and out. "So, you can hear me. Cool. My sister needs my help. She's been calling me."

"Angie? Little Angie?" I say, now interested.

"Yeah, she's only five."

I leave and go into the lobby, and he follows me.

"Whatever, dude," I tell him. "I don't care if I can see and hear you. I don't want to have anything to do with you. Stay away from me."

Now that he knows I can see him, he won't leave me alone. I find a spot between two older ladies and sit between them. "Finally," I say out loud. One of the ladies looks at me.

"Can you see me?" She quickly does the sign of the cross with her right hand still holding onto her rosary and starts praying.

There are people sitting on the sofas talking and sipping coffee. I notice some kids from school. That's a surprise, considering this guy is such a jerk. God, here he comes again.

"Dude," Big J says. "I know you hate my guts, but who else are you gonna talk to? I'll haunt you till you talk. I know... what song do you like? I can sing, too. Let me serenade you."

"Oh my God, dude, please don't sing."

He starts singing off-key. "Making my way downtown..."

Please not "A Thousand Miles."

I cover my ears. "La, la, la, la, la, la," I sing over his terrible voice, but it only gets louder. "Stop, please, for the love of Sweet Jesus, please stop," I yell.

He doesn't listen, but enjoys the song, "If I could fall..." He pauses for a second. "I've got... let's see... forever," he sings and then continues, "Tonight..."

"Fine! Fine, God Almighty, I know her. She saw me at the hospital. I couldn't believe it. She's nice to me, nothing like you. Is that what you want?"

Big J smiles. "Yep, I'm trying to get her to see me, too."

And for once, I get him. "Okay, so what do you want? Are you going to taunt and ridicule me here on this side, too?"

Big J gets into my face. "Hey, I'm sorry about all that. I was just trying to be cool in front of all of the others. It's hard for me to say, but I was... you know, jealous of you guys."

I gasp for air, as if I need air. "Jealous! Jealous of us? Are you kidding me? We're poor kids. We're on food stamps. You know, SNAP? We get free lunch. How can you be jealous? Y'all are the ones with money and nice houses. Your dad is the sheriff, for God's sake."

"It's not about money," he says. "Y'all are good kids. You care for each other and your family and friends. I never had that. My parents were always fighting at home. My little sister and I can't stand it. Now, I'm not there to protect her, and she and my mom may be in a dangerous situation. I just don't want anything to happen to her. My dad hasn't been himself lately, and I'm worried they'll get hurt. Everything is off at my house since the accident."

I turn and start to walk away from Big J.

"You hurt my brother," I shoot back at him. "Now he may be getting in serious trouble because of you. It never changes: people like you and your friends are always judging us. What are we going to do if your dad decides to go after him? You know more than anyone what he's capable of."

With a heavy heart, Big J lowers his head. "Look, I know this sounds crazy, but I'm here to help. I'm going to make it right, but I need your help."

"Why should I trust you?" I ask.

Big J does a quick check of the room. "Do you have a choice? Who else is there?"

I focus, zoning in on my spirit nemesis' eyes to make sure he's being honest with me, and something tells me his heart is growing. I picture it like the Grinch's heart, breaking through the mold. The tiny thing is slowly trying to fit into a crammed space.

"All right, man, but I'm watching you. We're good for now. You sure you're Big J? You are acting strange."

"Yeah, that's right. Thanks, Carlos. I have a lot of work to do. I'm going to be busy making up for how I acted, but I don't mind. I want to make everything right. I don't want my sister to end up like me. She's different, you know."

I sort of smile at him. "That's cool, maybe you can start by making sure other kids like you don't torment kids like my brother and me."

Big J walks over to where the sheriff is sitting and stares at his dad. "Don't worry, I'll make sure to handle my dad. In the meantime, I have to stop him from pressing charges against Cris."

"What? What are you talking about?"

"He has to pin the accident on someone. That's how my dad is. Oh, man! He may even get your dad involved. He's trying to blame everything on someone and that someone could go to prison, you know. He doesn't care who."

"No! He can't do that. Fix it, please. Are you out of your mind? He can't send my brother to prison. It was an accident. You know he didn't do anything wrong. You've got to stop your dad."

Big J jumps back a few feet, and his eyes lock with mine. "My dad feels like if he goes after Cris, it'll make him feel better. That's what I've heard him tell my mom, but she's not like him. I know Cris is innocent, so don't worry, I'll make sure my dad realizes it too."

"Yeah, you better," I say.

"Besides, I'm still dead. Nothing's gonna change that. And even dead, I may be able to do good for all of us," Big J says confidently.

Wow, this Big J has already figured out lots more than I have. Maybe he got a crash course or something. Not bad, but he still hasn't done anything to get through to his dad.

I hover around the front of the room and watch everyone. Big J stays in the back, observing… watching me. I think he's nervous someone may be able to see him. As I get right up front and stand next to the sheriff, I look down and notice Big J's little sister. She looks up at me, her eyes like magnets stuck to mine, and then she picks up her hand and sends me a tiny wave. Why is it she's the only one who can see me? Why can't Mamá or Cris see me? I'd love to talk to them and have them hear me. And why can't she see Big J?

Cris

I'm in the half-sleep before the waking fully-up-state when I hear Mamá rushing around our house, banging pots in the kitchen and slamming doors. I envision her waist-length hair, straight as a board, flying back and forth in a fury. Suddenly, she swings open my bedroom door and throws herself onto my bed.

"Hey, *m'ijito*, wake up! I'm going to pick up your grandmother at the bus station. Wanna come?"

The bus station is a ways off, in the city. It takes about an hour to get there and an hour back. I can use my time better.

"I'll wait here, Mom," I answer with my eyes still closed. "You go ahead."

"Okay, *m'ijo*," she says, kisses my forehead, walks out and closes my door.

I hear the birds chirping outside. All I had wanted was to meet my dad, and then out of nowhere, I found Selena. Now I'm getting a strange sense that she won't even want to acknowledge me. Nothing makes sense. My eyes get heavy. I grab the sheets and go back under the covers. Great, I think, I'll get a few more hours of sleep.

Tomorrow marks the three-month anniversary of the accident that took my brother's life, and every day we remember him. In this town, it was a big deal, and my mom needs my grandma around. A special Mass for my brother and the others will be offered tomorrow, but for now, I drift into Lalaland and go back to the night of the dance with Selena.

She's smiling at me with her head slightly tilted to one side, wearing my brother's letterman jacket.

In my mind, Selena and I are the only people in the room, even though there are probably a hundred others there. The music is heaven, enveloping us in our own little bubble, far away from the crowd. What is it about her?

It was her smile that drew me in, like seeing an irresistible soft puppy you have to cuddle. Thoughts drew me back to the tender kiss on her cheek, then on her ear, as she held my hand, and our eyes locked like we had finally found each other. No one has ever understood me, and she did. Selena knew my thoughts and my dreams without me saying anything to her. How could I feel this way about someone I just met?

As I start to wake up, I reach under my pillow, where I always keep my phone, check it and notice a message from Damian.

"I have scoop on Selena," his text reads.

Quickly, I dial Damian.

"Hey, what's up?"

"Have you checked Twitter?" Damian is big on social media. I don't like all that stuff. Sure, I check in now and then, but he's on all the apps.

"*Híjole, vato,* I don't think you want to hear this," Damian says in a shaky voice.

I sit up to pay close attention. "Spill, bro. What is it?"

"Well, I don't know how you feel about this, but... I think she's some kind of... witch or something."

"Shut up!" I jump off the bed, dropping the phone but quickly pick it back up.

"Seriously, she's into some weird stuff."

"Stuff, what stuff?"

"There's a video of her on Twitter, man. It's got like hundreds of likes, too. You should stay away, man. Consider yourself warned. Cris, are you there... Cris?"

Damian's talking a hundred miles an hour, and I picture his hands going at it full speed. For about thirty seconds, there's complete silence while I stare at the phone.

"Did you say witch with a W?"

"Yes! She's a witch, *güey*," Damian clarifies. "*Es una bruja*. You know, your mom is gonna freak. She's got the Virgen and crucifixes all over the house."

I hang up. It can't be true. As I stare at the phone in shock, it starts vibrating. Damian is calling back.

"No!" I yell at the phone. "That's not true. How can you say that?"

The blood starts to rush to my head, and heat overcomes me. She's like all of the colors of the rainbow blended into one. She can't be a witch. Damian's lost it.

"Take a breath. Let's think about this. *Cálmate*," Damian says.

"You're right, I need to calm down."

I pace around my room, but stop and stare out of the window. I notice a red cardinal perched on my windowsill. It stares at me for a brief moment as if it knows me and then flies away. But the cardinal soon returns and perches on a green leaf of the ivy wrapped around the tree branches. I can't stop gazing at its crimson feathers.

"Of course... there are good witches, aren't there? I mean, for everything bad, there is a good. Maybe... she's a good one. Maybe she has magical powers.... That's not so bad, right? I mean, look at *Star Wars*, right?"

"Yeah, look at what happened to Luke's dad. Whatever...." Damian says, trying to go along with me.

"We all have choices. Don't judge her, Damian. You don't know her."

"Yeah, well… let's wait and see."

"Cool. Selena with superpowers, like a superhero. That's not weird," I say.

My grandma sort of has magical powers. She does *limpias* and stuff. You know, *curandera* stuff.

"Shut up, Cris! Listen to yourself. You don't even know this girl. Do you want to see for yourself? What if she put some sort of spell on you or something? I bet that's what's happening to you. I've heard of the things they do." Damian waits for an answer then adds, "She gonna use you, man, and who knows what could happen? You don't need it. I'm your friend. I'm only trying to help you. Carlos isn't here to help you anymore. I am. Cris, you are going down a rabbit hole you may not be able to get out of. We've been down there, and it's not a place we want to be in. It's a dark, ugly place. Get yourself together."

The phone suddenly starts cracking up and dies. I try dialing back but the call does not connect. It still has juice. I dial back, still dead. I try again, and it finally goes through.

"Why the hell did you hang up on me, man?" Damian yells.

"It wasn't me," I try to explain.

I stare out the window at the light glowing in the yard and try to come up with an answer. "Hey, thanks, Damian, but I know what I'm doing. I don't think I need your help with this one. Besides, it doesn't prove anything." Click.

I get up, take a shower and try to get ready for Grandma's visit, but I can't even think. My mind keeps picturing Selena with a wand casting a spell. I shake the thought from my head. No way. That's not her. I met her. I met the real Selena.

I head to the kitchen to make breakfast and sit down with a hot cup of black coffee, inhaling its incense-like aroma and then exhaling it. Cradling the cup in my hands, I let the warmth soothe my nerves. I pinch my arm as tight as I can.

Nah, I think, definitely not. He's got nothing. I start laughing to myself.

A car pulls into the drive, and I hurry to the front door to greet Mamá and Grandma Blanca. I rush to open the door. Mom is carrying a suitcase, and my grandma is holding a large bag with all sorts of branches and weeds. Grandma is old but strong and is wearing a dark black dress that almost reaches her ankles. The dress matches her boring black loafers and black hose. She has her gray hair pulled back in a tight bun with big black bobby pins keeping it in place. She doesn't wear any makeup or jewelry. It's funny she's the mother of my mother, because they're so different. Mom always wears makeup and loves jewelry.

Grandma is the only person who can make my mom feel better besides me. That's what family is for, to help each other. Now we need her. If there is a time for Grandma to use her *curandera* talent, it's now. She was here during the funeral, and now she's back. Hopefully, she'll work her magic on Mom.

Grandma's clients call her a special healer. She can talk to people, read their future and see into the other world. She is spiritual and mystical. "Gifted," is what our family calls her. She was born with a special gift. All she has to do is touch a person or a piece of their clothing, and she can see and hear things no one else can. Some people just have it. Maybe that's what I need, especially now. A special gift to make sure Selena and I end up together. Now more than ever, I need to make sure we put an end to all this mumbo jumbo Damian is talking about. It can't be true. Grandma knows all about magical and mysterious things. She can help with Selena.

"*¡M'ijito!*" Grandma calls out to me as I reach for the handle of our front screen door. The birds are gathering around the front yard as I rush out to grab the luggage. The suitcases don't have rollers on them; they must be the only ones she's ever used. I place them down on the wooden floor and hug Grandma tightly, picking her up slightly.

"My baby's a good boy, *bien lindo. Mira cómo has crecido*, sixteen now...." she says, nodding at me.

"Grandma, I'm so glad you're here, but you really need to get some suitcases with those fancy spinners on them. You know we can get you some over at Wal-Mart." I place the suitcases from the 1980s down. I'm so excited to see my grandmother.

"*Qué* fancy *ni qué nada*. My suitcases are fine. I've been using them since your mother was *chiquitita*. But whatever you need, *m'jito*, I'll help you."

"Thank you, Grandma. I know you will."

Grandma places her arthritic hand on my shoulder and says, "*Te traje un regalo.*"

Swinging my arms and making my face wide with my stretched-out smile, I respond in song, "For me, what did you get me? Is it my birthday?"

With a wrinkled smile, Grandma turns and points out the window at a truck parked at the curb. "Go check, *ándale*...."

I run out and notice the passenger window is rolled down halfway. I peek inside and yell like a kid on Christmas morning. "Oh my God!" I pull out a gray puppy about five or six months old, wrapped in an old sack of potatoes. He's wiggling. "Grandma, how did you know this is what I've always wanted?" I hold him up to my face as the big pup licks my nose and cheeks.

"My neighbor asked me if I wanted him before I left. He needed to find a home for him. I knew this was where he needed to be." Grandma pets him and kisses him on his head. "*Es un lobo, le encanta la luna.*"

"*¿Lobo?*" Scratching my head, I try to remember what that means. I know Spanish, but sometimes I don't practice as much as I should.

"A wolf, *m'ijito*," Mom jumps in. "He looks like a wolf. He's a pretty big puppy."

"You hear that, Lobo? I guess you have a cool name now. My grandma just named you."

I take him into the house and create a makeshift bed for him with some old blankets in my bedroom. Then I lie down on the floor with him. Lobo immediately jumps out of the blankets and runs throughout the small house, and I laugh as he chases me.

My mom hugs me. "Thanks, Mamita," she tells Grandma. "I hadn't seen him laugh in a long time."

Grandma nods in approval.

I put Grandma's suitcases away in the bedroom, and we walk into the kitchen. With pans still on the stove left from breakfast and coffee bubbling in the pot, we sit down at the Formica table, the same table Mom and Rico bought when they first got married. I start pouring out three fresh cups of coffee. "*Ahora sí, vamos a tomar café, m'ija.*"

"*Negro para mí,*" Grandma tells me, as if I don't know how she always drinks her coffee.

She looks at me and smiles with her crooked half-smile and stained teeth, then turns to say a prayer over the coffee and does a ritual with her hands, ensuring that all the evil spirits are gone. Then, we relax and sip. She's always done that, as far back as I can remember. Neighbors used to ask her for help, and she would never say no. Gifted, some would say. Whatever you want to call it, Grandma was pretty popular.

Next, Grandma sets her coffee at the table's edge and places her wrinkly hands on the side of her chair. *"Ahora sí. Dime lo que les pasa."*

"*Es* Rico, Mamá," my mother blurts out without hesitation. She pushes her cup to the middle of the table and folds her arms. "He's trying to talk to Cris...."

If anyone knows the history with Rico and Mom, it's my grandmother, and she doesn't like any of it.

I take a deep breath and cut in on the conversation. "I need Dad in my life, especially now. I know I'll like him. He's a good person. He has to be. So much has happened. He can help me handle it all. Oh, I also met a girl."

Mom slides her chair away from the table, stands up and glares at me. "You don't know your dad, *m'ijito*. He's never been here for you."

Grandma gasps and agrees, "She's right, *m'ijo*. I know it's your dream to bring your father back and have him in your life, but sometimes things are best left alone. You have no idea what that man has put your mother through. Not once did he come around to see you since they broke up. Why would he want to see you now? I'm sorry, but that's the truth. He'll hurt her all over again, and he'll hurt you."

I reach over and take her hand. "Maybe it wasn't his fault. Maybe he wanted to be here. So much has happened to us... I want my dad in my life. Mom, please.... You don't understand. He's part of me. I need him now more than ever. Let's give him a chance, please, Mom."

Grandma nods her head, determined to do something. "You both need healing. That's why I'm here. I will help. *Es lo que hago. M'ijito*, I know you want to reunite with your dad, but he has a past you don't want any part of. He'll hurt you and your mother. Trust us. You don't know him!"

I wrap my arms around Grandma's neck and say, "I met a girl, and she's the best thing that has happened to me. She's like a piece of heaven, like a song written by a country artist just for me. It was the best night of my life at the dance. All I had dreamt of was meeting my dad, but then I met her, Selena, Selena Cano."

For some mysterious reason, Grandma takes my hand, places it on the table and grinds out these words: "I know this girl and her people. They're devils! *Pura gente mala...*" I can see her heart jumping out of her dress as she starts to pace back and forth in our tiny kitchen.

"Grandma, don't say that. I can't believe you're saying that. Why are you acting like that?" I look down at my hand

"It's true, *m'ijo*. They're *brujas. Lo sé en mi corazón.* I know these things. Stay away! I sense something..."

"No. Selena is sweet, and I fell in love with her. She's not a *bruja*. I think I need to talk to Damian. Why did he say all those lies about her?"

"Damian? Who is that, your friend? He can't help you. Cris, this is much bigger than you think. She's not who she appears to be. She's a witch, and it looks like I'm going to have to cleanse this whole household, including you and your mother. *Voy a tener que hacer una limpieza de toda la casa, de ti y de tu* mamá. *Traje todas mis hierbas y velas.* You may think my beliefs are strange or old-fashioned, but I have helped many people in the past. I have to help my own family now." She pulls her chair out and sits back down. "I have to take care of my family. That's what family does for each other."

"Great! A spiritual cleansing, just like in the Mexican movies or *novelas*," I say. My brows tense up, and I throw my arms up in the air. I don't blame them, but I don't understand.

"Cris, *no es juego*. This isn't a game. Tonight we'll do the cleansing, *la barrida*."

"That's tonight. But right now, I'm gonna go find Damian. He's the only one who makes sense right now, and he's lived in this backward town most of his life. Maybe he can help me figure something out."

"Bring him with you," Grandma shouts as I run out the door. "He can help us tonight."

"Watch Lobo!" I yell back.

Carlos

Mamá always told us Rico and she knew each other since they were kids. Cris and I always heard her talking to Grandma about our dad. I don't know how she could somehow throw him out like she did, but we never questioned her.

"*Tu mami...* was a beautiful girl and popular too," Grandma always said. "She became close friends with this girl, and trouble began."

"*Amá*, Cris knows what happened," Mom says.

"No, this is important. He needs to know the people he's dealing with. Tell him how it happened with you and Rico."

"Look, son, we loved each other, but after his brother died, he changed. He wanted to spend all his time with his friends. He felt sorry for your uncle's girlfriend because she went into a deep depression. We never saw him anymore."

Tonight, with Grandma as a witness, Mamá finally explains how their break-up happened. It seems Dad fell for another woman and one night, just like that, packed a suitcase and walked out.

"'What about the boys?' I asked Rico. 'Don't you care about them? They're only five years old. *Son inocentes.* They'll remember this day.'

"'They'll be fine,' He said. 'It's not the first divorce in the world. I'm not dying or anything; I'll be around. They can depend on me.'"

"Well... we don't need you," I told him.

"I know you boys knew far more than we realized. You were young, but gifted children. I could sense that there was something about the both of you that was different. Grandma knows what I mean. Once, I heard Grandma say she didn't want me to fall for someone from a small town and that she knew Rico had a dark background. I didn't understand. I thought Rico and I were meant to be together. Before he left, Rico did tell me, 'Make sure you give the boys this. It's all I have to leave him.'" Mom said Rico placed his suitcase down on the wooden floor and took off his old, purple and white letterman jacket. Some time later, I found this letter in the inside pocket.

Dear Carlos and Cris,

You're too young to understand what your mom and I are going through, but it has nothing to do with you. We love you both more than you know. You are beautiful souls, and no matter what, I will always be with you. Someday I hope you will forgive me.

I love you.
Your dad

From the conversations I've overheard over the years, I pieced together that Grandma tried to stop Mom from marrying Dad. Mom was so in love, she doubted Grandma's powers to pick up on the danger waiting for her.

"It'll never work," Grandma would say. "There's something about Rico. He's going to get in trouble hanging out with the wrong crowd. He has evil in him, I know it."

Maybe my parents were doomed from the beginning.

Grandma is at our home, and if anyone can see me, she can. All our lives, she's told us stories about how she can talk to spirits. She has a special room in her house where neighbors or relatives come for healing or to communicate with loved ones who have passed. She is the expert, the *curandera*. Cris and I always go along with the healing stuff, but talking to the dead... nah. We never believed any of it.

"Sorry, Grandma. Look at me now. I guess I'm a spirit. Do you hear me?"

Nope, no response.

"Grandma, I'm trying to reach you. I just want to talk to Mom and tell her I'm still here. I can't get through to her. Is it possible it's too soon. I need help. Can you hear me?"

Of all people, Grandma is the gifted one. I'm right here, but nothing, no response. I remember being at Grandma's house, when one of her neighbors came in for a session. Wringing her hands and playing with her wedding rings, she walked into the back room filled with candles, jars of herbs and statues of various saints. The statues were adorned with rosaries around their necks. Grandma closed the floral curtains, but I could still hear them. The prayers started, and repetitive chanting followed. The sounds would get louder and louder in rhythm as if in a song. Then there was sobbing and crying. Incense poured out through the curtains and made me sneeze. That's when I'd had enough and ran outside. When the neighbor walked out, she was smiling, as if relieved, healed and full of energy.

Dad is tall and lanky, not the typical football player type. His skin is light brown, like mine, and his eyes are brown, like mine. I do remember the day he left much clearer now.

"Just leave," Mom said, with her head down, looking at the wooden floor.

Rico looked over at her one last time and sighed deeply, knowing nothing he'd do could make the moment better. He opened the front door and walked out into the night as she stayed holding onto his jacket.

I knew what the jacket meant to him. It was his most treasured possession. He wore it all the time, it didn't matter if it was cold or warm. It was his comfort, his security. Mom didn't care, though. Not then. All she could think of was that he was walking out on us.

"I'll raise them by myself," she said, brushing away tears. "Millions of others have done it. I'm not the first."

With that, she let him go.

Our dad was gone.

Cris and I only had our mom after that. We never saw him again because, early the next morning, she packed up our belongings and moved us far away to the big city, where the rest of my family lived. Houston had much more to offer. It was a land of opportunity. Everything was there for Cris and me. And best of all, lots of family was there. That's what mattered. More than ever, we needed family. We would go back and forth between Moulton and Houston. We'd be fine.

Cris

I leave my mom and Grandma and call up Damian. "Where ya at?"

"At the diner. Come on over."

When I get to the diner, it's overcrowded with people. I feel a cold anchor in the pit of my stomach. Brushing away the cold sweat from my face, I take a seat opposite Damian. Every spot is filled, but everyone seems happy, drinking coffee and eating breakfast. Whispers of conversations can be heard over the mumbled voices coming from the TV mounted on the wall.

"I've been waiting for you. What took you so long? I thought you'd be here immediately when I told you." He's already drinking a Dr. Pepper and tucks his long hair behind his ear, pushing up his wire-frame glasses.

I lean back to get comfortable. "So, why are you telling me lies about Selena?" I stare him down as he reaches for his glass.

"Yep, she's a witch." Damian blurts out with confidence as he grabs his straw and starts messing with it.

"How can you say that? You don't know her. She's amazing."

"Full-blooded, man," he says, nodding his head up and down.

"Shut up, dude, just shut up! I think I fell in love with her last night."

"It's true, man. She's the devil. The DEVIL... and you don't want to go anywhere close to her. I've got proof."

"What proof?" I thrust my elbows down on the table to get closer to Damian, scrunching up my face.

"Some guys said they were messing around by the old cemetery behind her house and saw her out there. You know how some kids like to go hang out and party out there.... She was talking to someone in the middle of the night, but no one was there."

"That sounds crazy. Who said that? Do you know them?"

"It doesn't matter, but it was cold that night also, and she wasn't even wearing a jacket. They hid so she wouldn't see them." Damian sits back and slowly takes a sip of his Dr. Pepper.

"That doesn't prove anything." I can feel my face getting red.

"Maybe not, but they videoed her and posted it on Twitter. Everyone has seen it already. Everyone thinks she's a witch, man."

"Show me."

I pull out my phone, and Damian grabs it from me.

"Here, check it out... Apparently these guys, they go out there every night, and she's always out there talking to someone."

"This doesn't even show anything. It's way too dark. I have to go see for myself."

"Fine, let's go tonight. I'm telling you, though, she's scary."

I take a deep breath, "Wait. My grandma's in town, and she's doing this sweeping tonight to get rid of all of the 'evil' spirits around us."

"Hold on, hold on... she's sweeping out spirits?" Damian stops me for details, holding in his laughter.

"Hey, don't laugh. You know our culture, *vato*. Why don't you come with me, and then we can go to the cemetery?"

"A sweeping? I've never been to anything like that before. I think my mom has, but not me. Yeah, I'm in." Damian lets his laugh out and keeps drinking his soda.

"Well, it's a *barrida, una limpieza*. Same thing. Be at my house at seven."

"Cool, I'll be there. I can't wait to watch your grandma clean out the spirits."

I leave the diner alone, yet I sense someone walking with me. I stop, turn, but there's no one.

"Hello?" Nothing. I look up as if I heard something but nothing. I grab my arm and pinch it.

Yeah, I remember how things were so different in Houston. Yes, the kids singled me out, some were even bullies, but I didn't have to do spiritual sweeps on any of them. I never considered any of them to be *brujas* or *brujos*. If those kids only knew what I'm about to do, they'd freak. Maybe they wouldn't bully me anymore. Chills come over me as the hair on my arms sticks straight up. Something just passed by me, but I can't see anything anywhere.

"Is anyone there?" I stop and look around. Nothing.

Carlos

Seven o'clock approaches on the clock inside our living room, and the candles and incense are set up throughout the house. This is a nice touch. It smells like a church on a special occasion, with the thick burning smell escaping through the open window and filtering into the front yard. As Cris enters the makeshift chapel, Mamá and Grandma Blanca are busy getting herbs and branches together in the kitchen. He sits in the living room, surrounded by lighted candles. Lobo jumps up on his lap and rests his head down. I scoot in next to Cris, and Lobo starts wagging his tail and sniffing like crazy.

"What is it, boy?" Cris says.

Wow, pretty cool. He closes his eyes and tilts his head up, overcome by the experience. I sense his spirituality. Can he sense my presence? A connection with the flames burning on the wicks of the candles as they dance back and forth lifts my soul.

Knock, knock, knock, three loud bangs on the front door and Lobo barking bring Cris back to reality. He jumps up... unlatches the hook on the screen door and swings open the wooden door.

Damian bends down to pet the puppy. "Hey, who's this little guy, your guard dog?"

"This is Lobo. My grandma brought him for me." Cris picks him up and wraps him in his arms.

"So, he's a wolf?"

"Yeah. Come on in." He puts the pup down, takes in a big whiff and exhales it slowly, pushing the aroma toward his face.

"Woah, this looks like the chapel at church where my mom goes to light a candle sometimes. It even smells the same." Wiggling his nose, he continues, "I've never seen one inside a person's home."

"Well, now you have. I guess we weren't really using our living room, anyway. My grandma is pretty good at making quick changes. She's like a traveling *curandera*. Seems like she's transformed it into some sort of seance room."

Cris gestures Damian to follow him around the tiny living room taken over by candles and crosses.

Damian stops to sniff the candles and picks one up. "It's pretty cool. Vanilla?" he asks.

"You know," Cris looks at Damian and puts down the candle he's picked up. "I didn't tell you, but last night I had this weird dream about Carlos. He was at the dance with Selena, and he was wearing the jacket. He kept telling me something about an owl behind the white house. He asked me if I wanted to go for a drive with him and his friends. He said my deceased Uncle Carlos was with him. I didn't even know him, except for some pictures."

I walk over in front of Cris. If only he knew. That wasn't a dream. I was trying to talk to him.

"What did you dream?" Grandma asks.

"I know, dreams are so weird. An owl? Who would dream of that?" Damian laughs.

"No, don't laugh, no laugh…" Grandma Blanca warns as she approaches them. "No weird. It's him. *Es tu hermano*. It's your brother, *es* Carlos. He's with your *tío* Carlos. He's talking to you."

Damian and Cris look at each other. I stand right in front of them, but nothing.

Grandma continues, "Those are not dreams. They are visits... visits from the other side. If you are not careful, it can be dangerous. Visits let you know your loved one is doing fine after they passed. Sometimes, they have other messages for you, like a warning, be careful."

"Grandma, it was just a dream. That's it, just a dream. It can't be dangerous. I never even knew Tío Carlos. He died before I was born. I admit, though, his pictures kinda look like me."

Grandma reaches up to her hair, wrapped tightly in a bun, and tries to move it back and forth. "Yes, you look like him. And how would he know about your dance and about Selena? He contacting you, trying to tell you something. We need to find out what it is. Could be something good... or something bad. Only one way to find out."

With that, Grandma gets into her meditation mode.

"You can call him? Grandma, can you contact him? Do you think he knows something about Selena?" Cris shakes his head in disbelief, careful not to hurt our grandmother's feelings.

"I will try. First, we pray. *Vamos a comenzar. Silencio todos.*"

She starts humming and mumbling something to herself and making gestures with her hands. Damian and Cris blankly stare at her, mesmerized. Suddenly, the room fills up with some of my relatives and neighbors, including my mom. It's as if they all suddenly convened for this procedure, just waiting for Damian and Cris to arrive but they were there already.

"Join hands and form a circle," Grandma instructs.

With the candles glowing, Grandma Blanca begins her prayers. Everyone is holding hands. We form a circle. Grandma grabs the branches of herbs that are anointed with oils and homemade concoctions and starts brushing and sweeping them throughout the house while she chants out loud. The scents give Cris a brief sneezing attack.

"*M'ijito*, are you getting sick?" Grandma asks.

"I'm fine. I think the *hierbas* got to me, that's all."

Grandma Blanca then repeats her prayers a few times and then begins to sweep and brush everyone present, especially Cris, from head to toe. She goes to the front door, does the sign of the cross and brushes the door from top to bottom. She then wanders onto the steps outside and brushes them as well. Finally, Grandma walks over to Cris' pickup and chants and prays all around it. Then, she comes back inside. The look on her face seems to say, she is satisfied.

"Carlos, *ya está todo limpio. Estamos aquí con* Cris. Carlos?" she says, calling me directly.

I don't answer her. The room is entirely silent. There are no whispers, no creaks from the sofa, when the high school picture of me on the coffee table falls to the floor, shattering its glass. Everyone looks up, shaken from what has just happened. How could this happen? A picture doesn't just fall over on its own without anyone touching it or without any gust of wind. Even if it did fall, the glass wouldn't break, shattering all over the living room. Did I actually do that?

With all my might, I had willed the frame to move. It took all of my energy, but I guess it worked.

"Okay, Carlos, you have our attention," Grandma says as she reaches to pick up some of the pieces of glass, then stops as it cuts her finger slightly, making it bleed.

"Maybe it was the wind," Damian whispers to Cris.

I'm standing right next to Cris, but he doesn't notice.

"The door and windows are closed. There is no wind, no fan, no air conditioner," Cris says, his eyes wide.

"Carlos is here," Grandma announces, continuing to look blankly into the space of the living room as if in a trance, letting the blood ooze from her finger. She's the only one who senses me. I try my best to give her my message as she concentrates. Lobo runs up to the middle of the living room and starts barking uncontrollably at nothing. Then, he lies down and starts wagging his tail.

"Is it my brother? How do you know?"

In her trance, Grandma doesn't even hear Cris trying to talk to her.

"No one is going to hurt her. Don't worry. They are safe," Grandma says as if she were speaking to me standing in front of her. With that, she wakes up out of her zombie state, sweating and breathing heavily as though she had been running miles.

Mom rushes over to help Grandma. "Come sit over here on the sofa, Mamá. You need to relax, your blood pressure will go up." They sit down next to each other.

"I'm fine, *m'ijita*. Don't worry about me. We need to worry about Cris," Grandma says, turning to look right at me. "He doesn't want you to go near Selena or Rico."

"Grandma, you can see me, right?" I wave my hands in front of her.

Cris is freaking out. "What, why? Carlos, my brother? Did he say why?"

"He says they'll hurt you. They'll hurt your mother. He can't have that. He needs to protect you both. That Selena is up to something. Stay away from her," Grandma blurts out, then leans back on the sofa and breathes in a big sigh.

I stare directly at her and blow gusts of air onto her face. Her hair flies up a bit. "Grandma, what do you know about

Selena?" I ask. "Tell me so that I can help Cris. Is he in danger?"

She opens her eyes wide.

Cris goes over and squeezes onto the sofa next to her. "What? No one is hurting anyone. I love Selena. Of all people, Carlos should understand. He should be happy for me. Besides, he's dead. What does he care? He can't tell me what to do. That doesn't make any sense."

"Don't say that," Grandma orders. "They never die. They are always with us," she says and stands up, clenching her fists, and grabs a tissue to tend to the cut she had ignored.

Cris turns to our mother and begs, "Please, Mom, you don't believe this, do you?"

"*M'ijito*, your grandmother knows what she's doing."

"This is way off.... Grandma, you probably got it wrong this time. Everyone makes mistakes," Cris says, then grabs his keys from the nail on the wall and motions to Damian. "C'mon, Damian, let's get out of here."

"*M'ijito*, you can't mess with this. It's much bigger than you," Mom yells. "Please listen to Grandma Blanca."

"Mom, I love you, but sorry, I don't believe this stuff. I believe my heart."

Damian and Cris leave. They get into the pickup, turn the radio on, then start laughing with me right next to them. I try moving the knobs on the radio, but nothing happens. If they only knew what I know, they wouldn't be laughing. Cris may not believe in ghosts or spirits but he has to be open to the possibilities. I'm right here. I never believed in this stuff, but look at me now. Grandma is not wrong. She knows what she's doing. Something is up.

"Hey! Listen, you dumb jerks!" I yell in their faces.

Cris messes with the radio and turns to Damian, "Can you believe all that mumbo jumbo?"

"She's your grandma, man."

"That's all part of our culture and stuff, but I don't buy any of it. You know, we're in high school. We should know it can't be for real. I'll talk to the living, the real people, thank you."

They drive over to the diner. I smile proudly at my accomplishments and hear my ghost friend, Big J. He's calling me back to my bedroom. This ghost stuff is becoming easy, I realize as I magically appear in my room.

Big J is standing next to my picture, trying to push it over. "You have to teach me how to do that. I've been trying and I can't get it."

"You have to think about your loved ones, and it just happens. I don't know how… it just does. I think my grandma had something to do with it."

"Follow me. Angie needs our help."

"Okay, but remember that I need your help with Cris."

"Don't worry. It'll work out. Follow me."

"Have you seen your sister?" I ask.

"She's staying at my grandma's house right now. My parents are alone."

I do as Big J asks and find my new best friend hanging out in his old bedroom. We have transported ourselves to his house instantly. He likes to go there and think about what he needs to do. We can hear his parents arguing. They've done more and more of it since he's been gone.

Voices get louder and louder, like the sound of someone turning up the stereo full blast. Poor Angie. She's growing up with all of this. Her mom is crying with her head cradled in her hands.

"Nothing you do is going to fix it. Please just let it be," Big J's mom begs.

Mrs. Tanner is extremely pale and small. The wrinkles and hollow dark circles around her eyes show she's been through some tough times. She has shoulder-length hair that looks like someone flattened it on an ironing board. She's dressed like an old lady with a big dress that comes down below her knees. I can tell she's scared from how her entire body is shaking like a leaf. It must be terrible to live in fear of your own husband.

Sheriff Tanner looks like a grizzly bear with a big, brown, overgrown beard that apparently has been growing out for years. He's a giant towering over Mrs. Tanner.

Still, he yells and yells at her. "You listen to me. I'm the head of this family. I'm the one who makes decisions around here. If I want to do something, no one is going to tell me otherwise. Do you understand?"

Mrs. Tanner sheepishly nods her head yes.

"No one is going to find out about the pickup. Do you understand? As far as we're concerned, we found the driver of the third car and we're going to bring him in for questioning. It'll all be over when he goes to prison."

What is he talking about? Who's going to prison? Why is he threatening his wife like that?

"I don't get it, Big J. What's going on?" I ask.

"He's trying to frame your brother for our deaths. No one can stop him."

I didn't think ghosts could feel shocked, but I do. My blood is boiling. Oh wait, never mind.

"You know who babysits now that I'm gone?" Big J asks me. "C'mon take one guess. Selena, your brother's friend." Big J answers his own question. "My dad will hurt them both, and who knows what he'll do to my poor mom. She's not like him. I know what he's capable of. He's lost his mind since the accident."

It's just too much to bear. I go over to where Sheriff Tanner is yelling and cussing, about to hurt his wife, and I scream as loud as I can into his ear.

"LEAVE HER ALONE! YOU WON'T GET AWAY WITH THIS!"

"LEAVE HER ALONE! YOU WON'T GET AWAY WITH THIS!"

"LEAVE HER ALONE! YOU WON'T GET AWAY WITH THIS!"

Nothing. How could he possibly hear me? I rush over to the picture frame on the dresser and blow on it with all my might. I can't make it budge. Big J sees what I'm trying to do and joins me, blowing like crazy.

"I wish they would simply be happy. Why can't they be like normal people?" Big J asks me. "This was my everyday life. I don't even know why they got married. Now, things seem to be getting worse. Do you think they can work all this out for my sister?"

"He needs to be stopped," I say, looking around the room. An entire wall is covered with all types of guns and rifles. He is a sheriff, I guess, but it seems extreme.

Big J helps me to blow on the picture frame. Together we blow on it with all our might, like we're a windy hurricane in their bedroom. The gusts of wind start circulating and picking up faster and faster. The whirlwind lifts everything on the dresser and thrusts it all into the air, spinning and flying like a tornado. The picture frame falls to the floor and breaks with a loud crash! The yelling stops.

Sheriff Tanner turns around in shock, and Mrs. Tanner looks up from her cradled, bony hands. She looks around the room as if she senses our presence.

They stare at each other with a look they have never used before. The sheriff gets up slowly and walks over to pick up the picture frame, but as he does, he slips on one of the huge pieces of glass, accidentally slicing his bare foot. He falls on his back and bangs his head on the dresser. Blood starts to gush all over the floor. Mrs. Tanner runs to grab the phone and dials 911. She then grabs a towel from the bathroom and wraps up the foot, trying to stop the bleeding. He's biting his bottom lip with his eyes closed, trying not to scream in pain.

Mrs. Tanner sits down on the bloody floor next to her husband, who had just been yelling at her, making her cry, and now tries to comfort him.

"Help is on the way, don't worry. Everything is going to be fine."

He looks up at her and smiles. "I'm just trying to do everything for my family. You know that, right?"

"This is not just about us. We need to move forward. Angie needs us," she says.

I look over at Big J, and I know he's proud of his mother. We were just trying to get their attention. We didn't know he was going to get hurt. We didn't mean for that to happen, but look at them now. We stay close to them.

The ambulance gets to the house, and the Tanners are rushed to the hospital.

Big J and I accompany them in the ambulance and then at the hospital.

"It looks much worse than it really is," says the doctor. "The part of the foot he sliced bleeds profusely. We'll keep him overnight for observation, but he can go home tomorrow. He'll have to stay off his foot for a while."

Mrs. Tanner looks at her husband with hope in her eyes.

"This was a message," she says.

"You're right. It's a good thing Angie wasn't home. Yes, we lost our son, but we have to focus on our daughter. She's so young, and she needs us."

Cris

Inside the diner, Rico is talking to his regular customers about the local politics and sports and other usual small-town talk. Sitting at the wooden counter are three men around their forties and two ladies about the same age. They're all drinking coffee, eating some sort of pastry and laughing in between sips. The big screen TV mounted on the wall is on the news channel, but no one is paying attention to it. There are some booths with a few families sitting in them, and Rico walks over to them to ask them how they're doing.

"We're good. *Todo delicioso como siempre*, Rico."

"*¡Perfecto!*"

Damian and I walk over to an open booth and sit down. A waitress comes across and hands us a menu with "Rico's Diner" written on the top. The tall waitress has her hair pulled back in a ponytail and is not wearing a bit of makeup. She's strikingly beautiful. Her eyes are enormous, like cartoon eyes but in an attractive way. She's probably around our age, maybe a year older. As I grab the menu, our eyes instantly connect as if we understand things we've never recognized before. A chill goes down my back, making the hair on my arms stick straight up. I try to brush the hair back down with the palm of my hand.

"Do I know you?" I ask.

"I don't think so. You do seem familiar, though. Can I get you something to drink?"

"Just coffee for me. Black," I say.

"I'll have a Dr. Pepper," says Damian. "No ice."

She looks at him and tilts her head inquisitively.

"It dilutes it. I need the full effect of my Pepper," he says, then turns to look at the pictures on the menu, flipping it back and forth, running his finger through the selections, studying it closely.

"You know, you really should stay away from her," the waitress says with a blank face, looking right at me.

"What?" I yank up my head, placing the menu firmly down on the table. "What are you talking about?"

"Carlos wants me to tell you that. Do you know Carlos?"

Damian glares at me with wide eyes.

"Carlos? Did you know…" I ask her.

"Well, he's asking me to tell you to stay away from her. That's all I know, CC."

"CC…" Why did she call me that? No one calls me that except…

The waitress walks off and goes to take the order of another customer. What the hell?

I try to clear my head. My thoughts go back to Selena and the dance. I close my eyes to see if I can picture her. This town is exactly where I need to be. I found Selena, and my dad will hopefully be back in my life. What else could I want? So, why did this waitress say that?

The waitress comes back with our drinks.

"Sorry, what did you say?" I ask her.

"You should stay away from her," she says. "Cream, sugar?"

"No, thanks. I need all the caffeine I can get," I say, smiling at her.

What the hell is she talking about? I cross my arms to warm myself, pushing the hair on my arms down.

Damian is speechless. "Maybe you should listen to her, man."

"Are you going to order?" the waitress asks.

"Coffee, that's it. Do you know me? You're getting pretty personal here. Do you always talk to everyone... I mean, all your customers... like this?"

"Sometimes. If I get messages, I let them know. They usually thank me. I know her, well I know about her. Angélica, my name is Angélica."

"Okay, then, I'm Cris, and this is Damian."

"Her family's in some weird circle you don't want to get caught up in. She'll suck you in, and you won't be able to get out. Don't go there. Besides, Carlos is begging you to stay away."

"Wow. Weird circle? What does that mean? That could mean anything. Thanks for the advice, Angélica." I keep staring at her. I grab my arm while no one is watching and pinch hard.

"Sure, I'll be here if you want to talk. Remember what I told you." She spins around.

"Wait. What Carlos?"

"Your brother. That's his name, right?"

"How did you know that? My brother is dead. How can he be telling you anything?"

"If you want to talk, you know where to find me."

She touches my shoulder, and chills go down my arm and radiate throughout my body. She smiles at me and turns away to wait on another customer across the room and then she's gone.

"Woah, *vato*," Damian says. "Who is this Angélica chick? She acted as if I wasn't even here. Did you see that?"

"She's a waitress. Hey, sometimes they say strange stuff."

"How did she know about Carlos? And Selena?" Damian sips his iceless Dr. Pepper slowly. His eyes and nose follow the plates of burgers and fries passing by, landing at the neighboring booth. "You hungry, bro?"

"Maybe I'll order a burger, after all."

I watch my dad laugh and talk to the others in the diner out of the corner of my eye. He has to come over and talk to me, he just has to. Does he even know I'm here?

Damian gets up to go to the bathroom, and my dad comes over to our booth. "How you doing, *m'ijo*?" he says.

"Do you know me?" My voice is shaking, and my hands are sweating.

Rico sits down opposite me and looks me right in the eyes. Our eyes connect like magnets and stay stuck for a second. I feel a calm come over me. I don't feel nervous or scared, not even mad.

"I have always known you. I have waited years for this moment. *¡Gracias a Dios!*"

"Why, then? Why didn't you come find us?"

"*M'ijito*, it's so complicated. Your mom didn't want me near you, and I just wanted to keep the peace. I prayed that when you were old enough, you would come looking for me. Please forgive me, *m'ijo*. *Eres mi vida.* This diner is not much, but whatever I save is yours. I've tried to make it work for you. When you're ready, we can talk and try to catch up, if you're all right with that. It has been all I've wanted since the day I left. All I've done is pray for you."

He places his hand in his pant pocket, pulls out a worn-out rosary and holds it up to show me. "I have this here for you... praying every day for you. This is the same rosary I had with me the day I left. I promised I would keep it with me until I was reunited with you and Carlos. Here. Take it. It's yours," He says and hands it to me.

"I'm not even sure what to call you. Why should I believe you? You've never been around. You left the family, and Mom has suffered trying to raise us. As much as I've dreamt of meeting you, I have to think about her."

"Of course, *m'ijo*. I understand. I have tried, believe me. It was not possible. I never stopped loving you or keeping up with you and Carlos. I've always been close by." Tears roll down his cheek, and he wipes them away.

"Yeah, we can catch up. I'd like that. I don't know what Mom will say, though," I say.

Everything is going great for me. I have everything I want. Everything I'm praying for. Everything I'm dreaming of. It is all coming together. Finally.

"I have to go now. I'll call you," I say.

"Thank you, *m'ijo*, for giving me a second chance. *¿Un abrazo?*"

He stands up and walks over to hug me, and tears roll down my face, not from grief but from joy. I am finally going to start a life with my dad.

As my dad leaves, Damian comes out of the men's room and sees me heading toward the restaurant door. "Hey, you leaving already? No burgers? What did I miss? Did Angélica come back?"

"Yeah, she did, but let's go. I'll fill you in."

We walk out of the diner into the moonlit night. The stars illuminate the sky as if they were pasted there by an artist. Mom isn't going to believe this. Should I even tell her? Rico seems like a great guy. How could she have kept me from him all these years? Whatever, it doesn't matter now. What's important is I finally have my dad. And he wants to see me.

Unable to control my excitement, I rush out to go see Selena. Thoughts of Angélica pouring the coffee pop into my mind. Does she know something? It is so darn weird. Who is she?

Carlos

Cris jumps in the pickup and flips on the radio full blast. The windows are down, and his hair is blowing in the wind as the day begins to unfold. I sit on the passenger seat trying to talk to him.

"Cris, Cris! Please listen to me."

The roads are empty as he passes by the curve and gets to the stop sign where Big J and I lost our lives that terrible night. Cris pauses at the stop sign, as if trying to recall what exactly happened. The night is still, and no one seems to be on the road. The moon shines on the windshield, making him gaze up at it.

"I'm here, Cris. Open your mind. You can hear me. You can see me. You know you can."

He lowers the radio and looks around. "Did you say something?"

"No, man," says Damian. "I didn't say anything."

"*En el nombre del Padre, del Hijo y el Espíritu Santo,*" Cris prays, forms the sign of the cross with his right hand and finishes it off with a kiss to his thumb.

"For you, bro." He points up at the moon.

As he drives past the stop sign, the white house where Selena lives comes into view. There is a car in the long gravel driveway, and he pulls behind it, gets out of the car and walks up the drive onto the steps. He knocks on the door. "She's going to be surprised to see me," he says out loud.

A lady in an old robe opens the door. She has a cup of hot tea in her hand. In the background, the TV is on some channel with only static booming loudly. Two cats meow and rub their tails on her legs.

"Can I help you?" the lady asks.

"Good evening. Is Selena home?"

The cup of tea falls from her hand, and the cats screech in fear. She doesn't say a word and stares at Cris with a surprised look.

"Is Selena home, ma'am?"

"Please leave," she says.

"I just need to talk to her, please."

The lady's face turns blood red, and she slams the door loudly. Cris hears her locking it. Cris continues to stare at the closed door, confused, but doesn't leave.

"Hey there, you need some help?" a man's voice yells from the driveway.

Cris turns to see an older man in dirty work clothes holding a shovel. He must be a gardener or something. He has to know something.

Cris walks over to him and turns his back to look at the front door. There is no one there.

"Hi, sir," Cris says, approaching the man.

But the man turns around and starts walking toward the back of the house.

"I'm Cris," he calls to him. "Selena... I'm looking for Selena."

Nothing. The man keeps walking, ignores Cris.

"What? Selena's not here? Man, I get the message," Cris says to himself loudly and walks back to his pickup. "I don't even know your last name. Where are you, Selena?" He drives away with Damian. After he drops off Damian, he goes home where he scours social media sites for Selena, but nothing comes up. She had told him she didn't like any of it, not Instagram, Twitter, *nada*. She didn't even let him take a picture of her.

The next morning, Mom is not in the kitchen. There's no coffee.

"Mom? Where are you?"

Nothing.

"Mom?"

Quietly, Cris knocks on her bedroom door. "Mom?"

Nothing.

Cris slowly opens the door and peers inside, only to see a lump of covers on the bed. He goes to sit on the edge of the bed and pulls the covers off of his mom and gives her a kiss on the cheek and a hug.

"You okay?"

"*M'ijito*. I have a feeling only a mother can feel."

"I met him. He's great, Mom."

No response.

"Mom, I want to make it work with him. Please be happy for me."

"Rico hurt me, you know that, and I don't trust him. I never have after what he did to us. He ruined our lives. Where has he been? Now suddenly he's here and wants to be in your life. Does that make any sense, *m'ijito*? You know I always think of what's best for you and I try to protect you."

"Mom, maybe he's changed. Let me give him a chance. I need my dad in my life, especially now with what happened to Carlos. Don't be mad at me."

"You do what you have to do. I won't stop you, but I have a bad feeling about the whole thing."

"You won't regret it, Mom. He will come through, just wait and see. Please get up and get yourself together. This isn't good for you. Come on, let's get something to eat."

"*No tengo hambre, m'ijo.*"

"You have to eat, come on."

Cris pulls her by the arm out of bed and pushes her out of the bedroom. They walk into the dirty kitchen and sit at the table.

After a short while, Mom gets up and turns on the *comal* and heats up a couple of flour *tortillas*. She then spreads butter on them and sits down facing Cris. His soft eyes look into her sad, glassy eyes while he eats his *tortilla*, savoring the buttery taste. When he's done, he wipes his mouth with a napkin. I lick my lips remembering. There are dirty dishes in the sink, which is something he's not used to seeing. I sit down at the table and wonder if either of them will ever be able to see or talk to me, like Big J's little sister, Angie.

"Don't worry about the dishes, Mom. I'll do them. I have time."

"No, *m'ijo*. I'm fine now. I'll do them. You go and catch up with your dad, if that's what you want. He has lots to make up for. I'm sure he'll be telling you everything."

"Is there something you want to tell me, Mom, before he talks to me?"

"No. He'll have plenty to tell you."

There's a knock on the door, and Lobo goes crazy, barking into the air. Cris jumps up and walks to the door.

"*M'ijo*, don't answer it. I don't want to see anyone right now."

"Don't worry, I won't bring anyone inside."

Cris opens the door, and standing on the other side of the screen is Rico with a big smile on his face. He's wearing a nicely ironed white shirt with the words "Rico's Diner" embroidered on the pocket and dark blue jeans with cowboy boots.

"Dad? What are you doing here?"

Lobo runs up to him and starts growling.

"Cris, I need to talk to you. It's important. Can you go for a drive?"

"Hold on. It's all right, Lobo. This is my dad."

Lobo continues to growl.

"He doesn't know you," Cris tells Rico.

"Lobo, that's a strange name for a dog." Rico tries to reach down to pet the pup, but the growling gets worse, mixed with loud barking.

Cris goes inside and sees Mom bent over the sink washing the dishes. He leans over and kisses her cheek. "Mom, I'll be back."

"*Anda con Dios, m'ijito.*"

~~~

I accompany Cris as he gets into Rico's old 1980 Mustang. The radio station is on a classic rock station, the same one Cris listens to. "Cool," he whispers to himself.

"This isn't my car. I'm borrowing it for a while," Rico says.

"Where's yours?"

"Oh, it's in the shop. I have an old white pickup. I'm getting new tires. Look, I'm going to take you to my house to introduce you to someone, if that's alright. First, I need to explain to you what happened when you were a little boy."

"I'm listening."

"You see, your mom and I were kids when we met, and we thought we were in love. Then the accident happened, and she helped me get through the horrible time of losing my own brother, Carlos."

Cris crosses his arms and looks out the window as a flock of white birds fly into the sky. "I remember Mom telling us about Tío Carlos. She mentioned the accident but didn't like to talk about it. I know my brother is named after him."

"It was a long time ago. We were kids. Carlos was driving and was hit by an oncoming car. He was killed instantly. I have lived with the guilt. I couldn't have made it without her. Because of what happened to him, we ended up staying together, and if it hadn't been for that, we would never have had you. And look at you, son. I am so proud of what you have become. You're a smart, handsome young man. I'm so sorry I wasn't there for you. At least not physically, but I never left you, please know that."

"Still listening. You don't know anything about me. You don't even know what I want to do. Carlos loved football. He wanted a scholarship to play football in college. Mom told us that that's all you cared about when you were his age. You were able to follow Carlos' success as an athlete. But how about me. I have college dreams, too. I may not have a chance at a sports scholarship, but I'm one of the top students in my class. Did you know that? Did you know I like writing poetry and songs? No… You don't know anything. You have no idea who I am."

"How could I know if I haven't been there with you? Give me a chance, son. I'm here now. I want to know everything about you. I'll help you do whatever it is you want to do. If you want to write songs, then I'll help you. I know some people in those circles. I can make some calls. Let me first explain, though. During one of the fights your mom and I used to have, before my own brother's death, I was close friends with another girl. It turned out she got pregnant, but I didn't know until much later. When your mom found out, she couldn't forgive me. She kicked me out and never wanted to see me again. I don't blame her. I never blamed her, only myself. So, I made the best of this place in this small town and started over."

"But Mom always said that you left us...."

"Well, I think she believed, maybe still does. But I didn't... oh, maybe she's right... kinda..."

"Okay, Dad, I can see two sides to the story... but you never did come back to me and Carlos."

"Cris, again, you're right... and I'm sorry. But I hope you let me start over and make up for what I have missed, what I should have done."

"Dad, I need you... more than ever, now. I missed you more than you can know. And I'm willing to try for us to get to know each other and..."

"Cris, about getting to know me... I'd like you to meet a friend of mine and her daughter, who have become like family to me."

Cris exhales loudly and looks out the window again, trying to understand Rico's last statement.

I shout into his ear, "Bro, what is going on?"

He turns and looks at me. Can he see me?

He takes a another deep breath. "What are their names?"

"Lillith and Lilly."

Just then, they get to the stop sign where the accident happened, and Rico pauses and puts his head down. He does the sign of the cross.

"For you, Carlos. It never gets easier...."

They continue up the lonely road, and Cris sees the white house where he had been earlier that morning. The same car is parked in the driveway, but a small sports car is now behind it.

"I called and told them we were coming. You have to let them know ahead of time, or else you can't get in the door. Lilly's mom was never the same after the accident, you know.

It devastated her. I ended up spending lots of time comforting her to help her get through Carlos' death. They had plans. They were going to marry. You know... your brother was named after him. I wanted to keep his name alive."

"What happened?"

"It was Lillith. We found out she was pregnant right after the accident."

"And mom?"

"Your mom freaked out because I was spending so much time with her, you know, comforting her.... She never forgave me."

"I don't blame her. Are you..."

"She thought it was me who got Lillith pregnant, but it wasn't. It was never like that with us. Still, your mom didn't believe me. When I left, I came back here to be close to Lillith and, of course, Lilly, her daughter. They needed me, so I stayed close by."

"So, who is her dad?" I look at Rico in the eye.

He shrugs his shoulders and says, "Only Lillith can answer that."

Cris slams the window with his hand. "This is crazy. No one tells me anything!"

I look at Cris. "Brother, I'm finding this stuff out just now, too. They're all crazy. I can help you. Let me. Please open up." Am I getting through to him?

As Rico finishes his story, they pull up to the white house where Cris had been earlier. I can tell that a sense of doom is overcoming him. It takes over me, too. I want to run out of the car and scream as loud as I can, but no one will hear me. How can this be happening?

Rico gets out of the car and looks into the window at Cris. He knocks on the glass and gestures for him to come on out. Cris looks down at his hands as he wrings them nervously.

"Are you coming?"

"Yeah, I'm coming. Hold on," Cris says as he gets out of the Mustang and shuts the door. He stares at the white house as if paralyzed, then slowly begins to make his way up the steps.

Wind chimes are attached to the porch ceiling and are blowing harmoniously in the wind as they reach the door and Rico knocks loudly. Steps are heard approaching the door, and it slowly opens. On the other side of the screen is the same lady Cris saw earlier, but this time she's dressed up with her hair and makeup done, as if she's going out. She appears to be an attractive lady, for an older person. She looks nothing like how she looked earlier in her robe. He must have caught her at a bad time.

"Rico, it's so good to see you."

"Lillith, you're looking good. This is Cris. He's my son. Can we come in?"

She unlocks the screen door and opens it with a smile. She has large gold hoop earrings and a gold locket with an owl engraved on it on a chain around her neck. Her brown hair is straight and shoulder-length with some curls in it. She's wearing a sweatshirt with a Motley Crew emblem on it, and blue jeans and no shoes.

"Hi, Cris. You look like your dad. That's a compliment."

"Thanks, I guess."

Rico looks at Lillith and nods at her.

"I'll go get her. Please have a seat," Lillith says and leaves the room for a few minutes.

Rico and Cris sit down in the dusty living room. It is extremely unwelcoming and cold. Cris' leg is shaking uncontrollably, and he tries to push it down with his hand. He's biting his lower lip, and I catch him pinching himself.

"Things may not turn out the way you've imagined," Rico warns. "They never do, you know. Sometimes, they turn out better, though. You just have to wait and see."

Through the window, I see the same man from before with a lawnmower. Apparently, he's there all the time. Cris looks up. Standing at the edge of the living room, next to the sofa, is Selena. She's wearing shorts and a faded pink sweatshirt exposing her belly button. He immediately jumps to his feet, not able to contain his excitement.

"Cris," Rico says, "this is Lilly."

"It's Selena.... This isn't Lilly. What are you talking about?" Cris says, walking right up to Selena and looking at her right in her bright, blue eyes. "I've been looking for you. My God, you've been on my mind non-stop. I came earlier but couldn't find you."

When Selena does not respond, Cris stutters, waiting to see if she says anything....

"The jacket, I forgot...."

Selena abruptly cuts him off, pretending she doesn't know what he's talking about. "What do you mean?"

"Selena, don't you remember? I lent it to you last night?"

Turning away from Cris, she says, "I don't know what you're talking about."

"At the dance. Remember?"

"Sorry. I wasn't at a dance."

"I can't believe this. This is the girl I met last night. This is Selena."

"*M'ijo,* we better get going."

"I didn't even get your socials, phone number, nothing."

"Well, maybe it's because I wasn't even there." She nods her head and looks at her mom.

"Wow, unbelievable!" Cris utters, breathing heavily and pacing back and forth in the dusty living room.

"Cris, *vamos*. There's no sense talking right now," Rico insists and leads his son out the front door.

"No, how can she not remember? This doesn't make sense. Why is she acting like this?"

"Let's go, Cris," Rico steps out onto the porch.

As they begin to drive away from the house, the man mowing the lawn watches them like a hawk.

Cris turns around to keep an eye on him and sees him enter the house. "Who is that man?"

"What man?"

"The one with the lawnmower. Does he live here too? Is that Selena's dad?"

"*M'ijo*, I don't know who you saw, but no one else lives here. I've known Lillith since we were kids, and no one has ever lived with her except when she took me in for a while. No one else besides Lillith and her daughter live here. There was no man there. Lillith would never allow that."

"Whatever. This is getting crazy." Cris changes the subject. "Did you ever try to marry her?"

"No, it wasn't like that. She never loved me. We've always been friends, that's all. She needed the extra support after the accident. That's all it was. She got so depressed and talked about ending everything. Her family thought she was sick, unstable. My brother loved her. He would have wanted for me to look out for her and Lilly. I felt like I owed it to him, you know. He wasn't here to take care of them. I had to do it for him. After your mom kicked me out, Lillith was the one I'd talk to. She and Lilly became my family. We helped each other. Lillith had a troubled past with her father. He had been away in prison most of the time. When he got out, that's when the trouble began."

"What trouble?"

"He couldn't stand me and tried to get me out of Lillith's life. He claimed she had all sorts of dark secrets, evil secrets… and he wanted to expose her. She just wanted to keep the peace."

"Wow, that's sad. Grandma Blanca is here. I know I haven't given her enough credit, but this stuff is much bigger than us. We can't figure it out on our own. She knows about all this stuff, and we definitely need help. I'm becoming a believer in her work now."

"Well, I don't think your mom wants me anywhere near her or your grandmother."

"That's going to change. Be patient."

"Whatever you say, *m'ijo*."

Cris

Later that night, I'm driving with Damian, and he warns me again: "Remember what I told you about her. You really should stay away from her, Cris."

I grip the steering wheel tight. "Damian, you're my best friend, and I trust you, but I want to see for myself. If it's true, I'll give up."

It's already dark, and we park a ways off from Selena's house. The moon is bursting through the clouds and ready to greet the nighttime creatures. As we get down from the pickup, we can hear conversations coming from somewhere up ahead. Someone's out there.

Slowly, we pass the driveway and the white house and make it to the long yard behind the house. In the back, it's dark with only the light the moon gives off. There's a makeshift trail ahead, and we follow it to an old cemetery with broken headstones and overgrown grass. At a distance, we can see the figure of a girl in a skirt standing over a grave. We stop and watch to see what it is she's doing. She's reciting chants over and over while dancing.

Damian whispers and nods, raising his eyebrows, "I told you, bro. She's a witch!"

We stay back and observe for a minute, being as silent as possible. There are a few other people chanting the same words over and over. We can't make out what they're saying. They lift up some sort of chalice and spin around.

"Let's get out of here, *vato*! They're in the middle of some *brujería* ceremony."

We run back and get into the pickup, wiping the cold sweat from our faces and don't say a word for a few minutes. It's a lot to take in.

If only I could go back to only wishing I could meet my dad. That was all I wanted when we moved back here. Now, how did all of this happen? No wonder Mom tried to keep Dad away from me, what with his associating with witches. Regardless, he's my dad. Now, there is no going back. I have to face the reality of his past. Whatever it is, it is part of me. Damian rolls down the window to get air as he rambles on about Selena being a witch. He cranks up the radio. Santana is on, singing, "Got a black magic woman…"

I jump out of my seat. What the…?

"I want to go see my dad," I tell Damian.

"Dude, you don't really know him. You freakin' just met him. What's he going to tell you? Listen to your grandma, man. At least you've known her forever."

"Shut up, man. You were making fun of Grandma a while ago," I yell, trying to make sense of this witchcraft stuff.

"Cris, I've lived in this town for most of my life…. I was about four years old when we came from Mexico. I know it takes time to get to know someone."

"And… what's your point?"

"You can't tell how a person is when you first meet them. Sorry, Cris, but I don't know if you should trust him."

"Your dad's not the greatest either," I say.

"At least he's around. Even if he's always working, Cris. Dude, I'm just trying to help you."

I bang on the steering wheel. "No, not this time. I have to see my dad. He's the only one who knows what happened."

I glance at my friend. He's a statue, but I know he'll be fine. In about a minute, he'll start up again.

We drive over to the diner. A closed sign is on the door.

"That has to be a sign, don't you think?" Damian says, hoping that's the end of it.

I back up the pickup nervously, turn it around and head toward the adjacent apartment, determined to talk to Dad.

"His place is around the back. Let's go, he won't mind."

Damian hits me on the shoulder. "Of course, he won't mind. I knew you'd say that. Are you losing it, Cris?"

We drive around to the back of the diner, and there's a small apartment with stairs going to the top floor and a 1988 red Mustang parked out in front.

"That's it." We get out of the pickup, climb the dark, creaky stairs and knock on the door. Rico answers almost immediately, still wearing his blue shirt with "Rico's Diner" embroidered on the pocket.

The door opens and Rico is holding a glass of soda with bubbles still unsettled. He had probably just gotten home from the diner because he apparently didn't even have a chance to change, when he heard us knock at the door.

"*M'ijo*, come in. I'm so happy you came. Come, sit down. Who is your friend?"

"This is my best friend, Damian."

"Welcome, son, come right in. Is everything all right?"

"No, not really." I scan the inside with my face flushing and the veins in my neck straining to pop out. "Ever since I tried to meet you and ever since I met Selena, everything has been strange, Dad. I don't understand it. What's going on with everyone?"

I stand at the door, looking around his tiny apartment. There's not much to it. There's a beat-up sofa, a TV, a coffee table and a small table with mismatched chairs in the kitchen.

Rico clears his throat and steps toward us.

"The weirdest thing just happened to us," I continue. "Not weird, but super weird. Dad, you need to tell me everything you know about that girl, Selena, the one you call Lilly. Are you involved in something I should know about?"

"Calm down, *m'ijo*. I'll tell you whatever you want to know," Rico says.

"Why was she dancing at the cemetery? Who were the guys she was dancing with? And why did she pretend she never even met me?" My words spill out.

"*M'ijo*, Selena's mom is not well."

"Is she sick?"

"You met her. She has problems dealing with everything that happened, and it has taken a toll on her. Unfortunately, Selena is the same way."

"You're saying Selena, *my Selena*? What's wrong with her?"

"Well... she can be perfectly fine one day, and the next, she's a totally different person. I've been trying for years to help them. Lillith refuses help, but Selena is more receptive." He pauses and nods his head slowly. "She goes to therapy. Sometimes it's group therapy with young people and adults. It helps. The kids in her group have become her friends, and sometimes they come over to her house. They like to hang out at the cemetery."

"I don't believe you!" My face gets hot and I'm sure it's bright red by now.

"You don't have to believe me. I'm telling you the truth. She hangs out at the cemetery sometimes."

He tries to place his hand on my shoulder, but I shake it off.

"So... is she a WITCH?" I pull away from him.

"They're kids. You know kids. Y'all are kids."

"We don't dance on people's graves or chant weird stuff." I grab my arm and pinch it as hard as I can.

"Look, *m'ijo*, you haven't been here for years. You can't expect to catch up on everything right away. It's going to take time. Everyone has a past. Everyone has a story. Some people's stories are more colorful than others. Ours, I guess... has been a bit colorful." Rico grabs a chair from the kitchen table. "Here, sit down. You, too, Damian."

"Look, I'm not here to visit right now," I say. "I need answers."

I scoot back and forth on the unstable chair and then stand back up. He looks over at Damian, who is standing by the door with his arms crossed.

"Maybe we better get going, Cris," Damian says, almost begging.

"Hold on... I don't even know who Selena is. Why won't she talk to me now? Because she found out you're my dad? Is she a witch? You know... that's what the rumor is, right, Damian?" I look at Damian for back up, not sure what I'm going to tell him. "What the hell, Dad? Who the hell is Selena and why did you call her Lilly?"

"Cris, listen carefully. Selena's mom was in love with Carlos, your *tío*. Yes, I believe Carlos was also in love with her, too. He was killed in an accident before you were born. Everyone's lives were ruined. I moved in with your mom, and then you and your brother were born. You all were the only good thing that happened to me. And, Lillith, she was never happy, she kept calling me, needing me to help her get through the trauma of my brother's death. Your mom kept telling me she couldn't trust me, thinking I was having an affair with Lillith. I wasn't. It wasn't like that, but your mom never believed me. I finally had to leave. The accusations were too much. I couldn't take it. I regret it now, but that's what happened, and I can't change that."

"So why was her dad in prison?"

"That had nothing to do with us. I'm afraid I don't have those answers."

We leave Dad's apartment, and the night seems even darker than before, with the moon slightly grinning at us. Damian is in the pickup looking at me like I'm some psychopath. He's the one who started this whole witch thing, anyway, so now we're going to go back to talk to Selena. The pickup is old, but I'm lucky I got to drive at fifteen. We sit in the truck for a moment, and I try to think as Damian stares out the window.

"Is she even worth all of this, man?" he asks. "She's just a girl.... Why is she so special? I mean, you barely met her."

I turn and look at Damian. He's not looking at me. I pinch my arm and start the engine. "Yes, she's worth it," I say.

"Okay, okay, already.... Let's go back and see if we can talk to her. Your jacket, bro? Did you ever get it back?"

"No, I have to get it back." If nothing else, at least I'll have my brother's protection with me. Maybe I shouldn't have lent it to Selena. What was I thinking?

"No, she never gave me a chance to ask for it. She was all weird when I saw her."

"Well, you can ask her for it now."

We arrive at the house and walk up the steps to the front door. The wind chimes hanging from the porch ceiling are swaying. I knock. We look at each other and wait. Nothing. We knock again. Nothing. We step back and walk down the steps and look around the side of the house. Nothing. The sound of the wind chimes gets louder. The gusts of wind blend in with the rhythm as if they were playing a familiar song. I'm trying to make it out but can't quite figure it out.

"Well, I guess no one's home," I'm ready to give up and come back tomorrow.

"Let's walk to the back," Damian suggests, a little hesitant.

"You think they're back there? We can't walk into their yard. That's trespassing, isn't it?" I question.

Nothing ever good happens when you walk to the back late at night. I've seen too many horror movies to know that.

"Well, that's where the cemetery is, right? Let's try."

"I don't know... Oh, I guess we can check it out. What the hell, we're already here." Damian nods in agreement and, hesitating a bit, follows me.

We start to head out through the makeshift trail leading to the old cemetery in the back of the house. Then, we begin to hear chanting and singing. I eagerly walk ahead of Damian. Of course, I want to find out about Selena. It's very dark, and we use the flashlights on our cell phones to see the trail in front of us. Thank God we still have power.

As we get closer to the cemetery, the chanting gets louder. We slow down to see what is going on. In the distance, there are girls dancing with two boys who are holding candles in their hands. One of the boys is wearing a letterman jacket. Could it be the jacket I lent Selena? As we slowly approach, the dancing stops, and the figures disappear into the night. We hear a whistling up ahead in the darkness.

"Selena? *Helloooo*, Selena, is that you?" I call out softly. I can see her pretty clearly now.

"What are you doing here, and why are you here?" She asks, in a calm, nonchalant voice.

"We thought we'd join you. Is that all right?"

"No, you can't. I have to go inside now. I'm not supposed to be out here."

"Who was here with you? Where did they go?" I get closer to Selena, and she backs up.

"No one, just me."

"We saw them. Right, Damian? There were two other guys here and another girl. Where did they go? One of them had my jacket."

"You're imagining things. Y'all better leave."

"Hold on. Let me see something," I say and look over at Damian.

He grabs my arm. He can probably feel my goosebumps.

I stutter. I'm struggling with words. They're stuck in a lump in my throat. I can't swallow.

"Come on, Damian."

His face is white. I'm frozen for a moment.

"Cris, did you hear that noise?" he asks. "In the trees? Were they…?"

We walk up to the grave where Selena had been dancing. Laying over the headstone is Carlos' jacket that I lent her. There it was, perfectly cradled over the marble headstone as if it had just been taken off. I shine my phone light on the headstone and read the name out loud.

Carlos Pérez
Born: January 15, 1982
Died: May 30, 2000

Damian looks over at Selena with eyes wide open, then looks at me, then back at Selena.

"Who are you? Do I even know you?" I ask her.

"I'm Lillith, just like my mom. Carlos has been trying to tell you something. You need to pay attention."

The phone drops out of my frozen hand and I quickly pick it up. "Let's get out of here, bro. NOW!" I scream at Damian.

Selena comes up to me as if in a trance. "What's the matter, Cris? Don't you know who I am? Don't you want to talk to us?"

As we run back through the makeshift trail we hear screeching noises in the trees.

"*Lechuzas*? Did we hear owls?" I quickly do the sign of the cross and tell Damian, "*Güey*, I'm moving back to Houston. This place is too weird."

I grab my keys from my pocket, and they fall out of my shaky hand onto the tall grass. "*Híjole*, now what?"

Damian comes over and picks up the keys. He hands them to me. "Cris, calm down. We'll figure this out."

It's like we're in a scene of a scary movie. We race into our pickup. I quickly turn on the ignition and put the truck in reverse. I try to put everything together in my head, but nothing makes sense. As I reverse into the street, a figure gets into a truck parked next to us and drives off.

"Let's follow them. Let's find out who that is," Damian announces, even though he's still shaking from seeing Selena or Lillith or whoever the hell she is.

It's a dark-colored, old pickup, but it's nighttime and we can't tell the exact shade. Damian leans over to look at my speedometer. "How fast are you going? You're going to lose 'em. *¡Dale!*" Damian is practically pushing the petal to try to accelerate. I shove Damian away. "I'm not going to force my truck to go any faster. Besides, the cops will stop us. I don't want Sheriff Tanner to catch me speeding or chasing someone. He'll throw us both in jail. You know that. He hates us." The sweat on my forehead is starting to drip down the side of my face while I grip the steering wheel tightly.

"He's gonna get away, *güey*. No one's around. Floor it!"

Thankfully, there isn't traffic on the road. I focus and hit 50, then 60, and the dark pickup is back in sight. The driver takes a sharp right and drives to the outskirts of town, and we keep following.

"What are you going to ask him when he stops? What if he has a weapon or something?" I ask Damian, who has opened the glove box and is digging through it. I'm not sure what he thinks might be in there that can help us.

"What are you looking for?" I reach over to close it.

"We have to be prepared," Damian says. "Don't you have anything I can use for protection in here? Besides, I'm not asking anything. You're going to find out who he is and what he's doing at Selena's house. C'mon, you were madly in love with her yesterday."

"Yeah, that was before I found out she was some sort of witch. Do you really think she's a witch?" Not taking my eyes off the road, I think, *Witches aren't always bad. Grandma is kind of like a witch. She helps and heals people like good witches do.*

Damian nods. "Yep, she's probably for sure a witch, but so what. You need to talk to her."

I glance out at the empty fields passing us by and the radio suddenly turns on full blast.

"Hey, I'm trying to concentrate here. Turn it down a bit." I grip the steering wheel tighter.

"I didn't touch anything," Damian says.

I reach over and turn the radio off. "What's wrong with you!"

"Oh, shut up! I didn't even have the music on because I was freaking out."

The dark truck is now entering an old dirt road leading to a barn surrounded by cornfields. We see other cars parked along the road. There's a corn maze. It used to be a popular hangout.

"Pull over, let's figure out what our next move is," Damian suggests.

I park close to the barn entrance and see a man get out of the pickup, walk to the barn door and close it. Again, the radio blasts, *"Amor Prohibido"* by Selena. We look at each other and at the radio knobs. I reach over and turn it off, but then it turns itself back on, playing full blast.

"What the heck is happening?" I scream.

"I think she may have put some sort of spell on us or something. Turn it off!" Damian screeches, out of breath.

"No, it's not a spell," I say. "It's Carlos. He's trying to talk to us. Listen to the song."

I turn the radio up loud again.

My brother loved that song. Mom always told us her and Rico's love was not meant to be.... It was prohibited: *"prohibido."* She played that song since we were kids. That was my parents' song, but their love was not possible. Only Carlos knows that."

"You think Carlos is here? Man, this is getting creepier!"

"Be cool, man. Don't you see what's happening? This is real."

"All right, all right. I guess I've seen enough weird stuff tonight to believe this, too."

We step out of the pickup and start walking toward the old barn. We see a sign on the fence that reads, "Keep Out!" We pick up our pace, but I trip on a corn stalk thrown in the middle of the path and quickly pick myself up, dusting off the dirt and grime. I focus on the light coming from the entrance. Damian follows.

As we approach the barn, we can hear music playing. We finally get to the barn door, and as we open it, a man greets us and says, "We'll be closing in a little while."

"That's okay," I tell him, "we'll only be a few minutes."

The large interior of the barn is bustling with teens, music and pizza. Laughter and loud conversations engulf the party. As I catch my breath, my eyes scan a corner of the space by the snack bar. A table crowded with kids, covered with drinks, food and strange-looking objects bustles. I notice Selena smack in the middle, laughing with "her friends." I have never seen any of these people before. Where did they come from?

"Hey, Cris, do you know any of those kids?" Damian asks. "Who the hell are they and where did they come from?"

I turn to Damian, knowing we're out of our territory. I push my hair behind my ear, shake off the dirt from my clothes and lead the way to Selena.

"What the… Selena, what is all this?!"

"Just a little get-together," she says, flashing me an evil smile.

"Why didn't you say anything? You didn't tell us you were coming over here."

"Calm down, Cris. We're merely having a little fun. Don't you like to have fun?"

"Something super strange is going on here. I don't like it."

Damian sits down next to her and stares at her friends. They glare at us, shaking their heads in disapproval.

Damian scoots right up close to her, almost touching her wire-frame glasses, and says, "This is all your fault! It will always be your fault. I'm going to find out what you're up to."

The lights flicker.

A booming voice comes over a loud speaker: "Okay, everyone, we're closing."

Everyone stands up as if playing a part in a school play, pushes their chairs perfectly under the tables and meanders toward the exit. We leave the barn behind us, walking alongside Selena's group.

"I don't trust you, Selena," Damian says, menacingly.

"Don't worry, Damian, it's not what you think." Selena winks at me.

"I'll find out what's going on with you," he yells. "You can't hurt my friend!"

Just like that, Selena disappears into the darkness.

"Don't worry, Damian. Believe me, it's not what you think," she repeats from the shadows.

"Oh, I'm pretty sure I know what this is," Damian calls out to the darkness.

I walk toward the pickup with my head down, kicking the dirt and mumbling to myself. Damian rushes to catch up and grabs my elbow.

I jerk it away. "I don't feel like talking." I keep walking slowly.

Damian catches up again. "Maybe she's telling us the truth. Maybe she's not a witch… maybe she just has some freaky strange friends."

Combing my hair back with my fingers, I say, "*No sé…* I wish Carlos was here. He'd know what to do."

Right as I say that, a small white sports car pulls up next to us. The window rolls down, and the driver is wearing a cap. She turns to us and signals for us to get in. It's Selena.

"Hurry up, we don't have much time," she says.

I quickly look at Damian for his reaction, and without hesitation he runs up to the car.

"C'mon, dude. Let's go," he says.

We jump into the vehicle and peel off into the darkness, passing the empty roads with mist clouding the windshield.

Selena throws off her cap, and her hair cascades down her back. Neither one of us seems to be shocked that Selena is driving us both to who knows where.

"Where are we going?" I finally ask.

"I have to show you something," Selena says, staring into the mist in front of us.

In all of my daydreams of getting together with Selena again, never in a million years would I have imagined it like this. She would never have been a witch. She definitely wouldn't be involved with my dad. Who is this mystery girl? The more I think about her, the more she fascinates me. I watch as she holds the steering wheel at the ten and two position, tightly focusing on the road. Her curly brown hair has new blonde highlights in it and looks incredibly glamorous. She tosses it over her shoulder and glances at me, smiling. Damian is sitting in the back seat unbelievably quiet. He's probably giving me time to figure out what's happening.

I can't help but inhale the floral scents permeating from her hair.

"Where are we going?" I ask again.

"If I told you, you wouldn't believe me. I have to show you and your friend. You have to trust me. Believe me, please, I'm trying to help you. I didn't ask for this, but I have to do it."

I sit up straight and practically yell, "Help us?! Are we in trouble? Please tell us what's happening?"

Damian grabs the back of my seat and sticks his head into the front-seat area.

"Yeah, what the heck is this? Did you just kidnap us?" Damian asks. "¿Qué onda, Selena? Take us back!"

She jerks her head around to face Damian and says, "You both came on your own free will. I didn't force anyone to get into my car, so shut up and stop freaking out!"

Damian gets quiet for a few seconds, then says, "Chill, Selena. Watch the road! You're weaving all over the place!"

Selena hugs the steering wheel. "I swear I'm not doing it. It's like I'm fighting to control the wheel. Someone is here with us. Stop!!!"

Damian and I look at each other and say nothing.

"Look, up ahead there's an auto shop that belongs to a friend," she says.

"So, what do we care about an auto shop in the middle of nowhere?" I ask, looking at Damian so he can agree with me.

Selena slows down and stops on the side of the road and the shop seems abandoned. "Listen. I asked if his friend could check out my car. He said I could leave it here tonight, and they'd take care of it first thing in the morning. No one is here right now. They only work in the day. We need to hurry, someone may try to stop us again."

The auto shop is an enormous shed made of silver-looking side panels. I don't remember ever seeing it before.

Selena gets out of the car and starts to head around the side of the building. "Let's go."

We follow. It's pitch dark except for a light in the front of the shop, where bugs are buzzing around. The light starts to flicker, then blinks on and off, faster and faster. The flickering gets stronger with popping sounds and then the light turns off.

"I told you, we better hurry," Selena says.

Using our phones for light, we walk the length of the shed, make it to the back, where we see a sliding door with windows on the side.

Selena points ahead for us to try to get in.

I take a step back. "Oh no! We're not doing that!"

She pushes me forward and taunts, "Don't be a chicken, c'mon."

She reaches up and tries to slide one of the windows open but can't get it to budge. She tries again. "It's not locked." When it moves a tiny bit, then shuts back, she shouts,"Ugh! Who is doing this?" Then, with all her strength, she yanks the window open.

"What are you doing? You can't go in there? Are you crazy?" I whisper-shout.

Before I can say anything else. Selena pulls herself up through the window, jumps into the building and calls to us, "C'mon! Jump in! Are y'all scared or what?"

"Well…" I shrug my shoulders at Damian.

We follow her lead.

Damian goes in first and looks back at me. I hear a loud thump.

"If anything happens, it's on you, bro," he says.

I climb onto the windowsill, look around and jump down into the shed and join Damian and Selena in the darkness. My nose tingles with the scent of car paint, oil and rubber tires, and it's starting to nauseate me. A few cars are up on lifts. Along the side walls there are shelves and shelves of tools and paints. Off in a corner is an office with glass windows. The fading color of the concrete floor has cracks and streaks of paint and grease. I feel like coughing with every breath as I inhale the fumes. I shield my nose with my elbow.

"Great, now do you all feel like superheroes?" Selena asks as she flexes her muscles.

I shake my head as my brain scans the place for an exit. "You can be the hero, we're good."

Pulling out her phone from her pocket, Selena explains, "I don't want to turn on the lights and draw attention to us, so I'm going to use my phone."

Using the light on her phone, she walks us over to the back, where there's a pickup covered with a huge old tarp.

Suddenly, her phone dies. "Dadgummit!"

She reaches her arm over to me and then to Damian, "One of you, turn on your phone light."

"Here you go!" I say and hand my phone to her.

She points it toward the back."What's this?" Selena asks, pulling off the tarp from what we see is a gray Ford pickup truck.

Looking at me, she inhales. "Cris, this is the third car." Selena says this as if she's been holding onto to the worst evil secret in the history of the world.

"The pickup was white," she says. "They painted it. Check it out. You know about cars."

I look at the car then at her, "Yeah, I know cars. So, what does this mean?"

"Big J's dad is trying to frame you or your dad. I'm sorry…"

My mouth is open so wide, I can't even get my words out. I can't believe what I'm seeing.

"Why is he trying to frame us?" I finally ask.

"He's been trying to keep my mom and me away from your dad. He's never trusted or liked Rico. He's close to my mom. He's always hanging around. When he found out about you, he got worse. He's threatened Ms. Tanner that if she said anything… but we know the truth."

"Wow, no wonder Big J was such a bully," Damian says, shaking his head.

"I've heard Sheriff Tanner and his wife talk about it. I don't think the Sheriff intended any of it to happen. Maybe he was trying to stop Big J or maybe he wanted to cause a small accident to make it appear like you were at fault. Of course… I really don't think he thought anything would happen to anyone, especially not to Big J." Selena looks down and then continues, "I'm so sorry it all turned out like this. I had to distance myself. I was trying to find out what was going on so I could help you. Please understand."

Looking around in all directions, Damian says, "We have to go to the police. He can't get away with this. That jerk!"

"What are you talking about? He *is* the police," Selena says.

I take a breath. "No... we can call Felix. He can help us."

I pull out my phone and start taking pictures of the pickup from every angle. I take pictures of the shed.

Damian points toward a door. "Let's check out the office. Maybe there's some clue in there."

"No, I don't think we should do that," I say. "We've already done enough. Besides, it's probably locked."

We go up to the office door and try wiggling the door handle. Sure enough, it's locked. We peer in through the glass but can't see anything.

"My aunt, my mom and I all heard him talk about it. I have proof," Selena says.

We leave the office and start walking toward the open window, trying to leave quickly when a gust of wind slams it shut.

"Oh my God, J! Stop!" she shouts as if talking to someone, then looks to us. "Help me open this, guys. I think I'm making him mad."

I rush up to Selena. "What are you talking about? Who's getting mad?"

Her eyes are wide, and she's shivering. "He's here. Sorry, he's trying to stop me... but he can't."

I stand in front of her. "Who's trying? You're acting weird, Selena."

"Let's get out of here," she says.

"You did the right thing, Selena. Thank you," I say. "Now, we have to call Felix." I place my hand on her shoulder and reassure her.

"Felix?"

"He's the local police officer and a family friend. Felix is the best cop in town. He's like a brother to us. He'll help us."

We climb back up to the window and jump down to the ground. We make our way quickly around the side of the corrugated metal building. The mist is thicker now, and the breeze is much cooler. We get into the sports car and drive back toward Malton.

I scroll through my contacts, find Felix and dial.

He answers right away, "Hey, *amigo*, what's going on?" He says.

"Felix, I need your help. Can you meet me," I ask.

My voice shakes, and I swallow big gulps of air as I try to talk. Felix knows something serious is happening. He gave me his number to call him in case of an issue, but I rarely do. He'll know what to do.

"I'll be off in about thirty minutes. I can swing by your house."

"Thanks, I'll see you then."

I put away my phone, and in the back of my mind, I see Carlos nodding at me. Did he know?

"Drive to my house," I tell Selena. "He'll meet us there."

"You have to tell him everything," I tell Selena.

"I'll do it. Believe me. If anything, I'm a good witch, not a bad one."

"Hey, that was Damian who thought you were evil, not me. Blame him."

"You still have a lot of explaining to do as far as I'm concerned," Damian says, "but we'll talk later."

Carlos

Something is up with my so-called new best friend. Once an asshole always one. Grandma taught me better, and I should have followed my instincts, but, hey, my brother will figure this out. I tag along with Cris, Damian and Selena as they head over to the auto shop and, sure enough, Big J's coming along for the ride, too.

I'm squeezed in next to Cris. I don't take up any space. "What are you trying to do? Leave them alone, jerk!" I yell at Big J, who is trying to take over the steering wheel.

"Oh, by the way, friend, thanks for helping me figure out all this ghost stuff. I'm getting pretty darn good at it," he says, laughing at me.

Selena is speeding down the dark narrow roads toward the end of town, where Cris never goes. As she drives, she's arguing with Damian, who's sitting in the back seat. He's totally enjoying it.

I try to mess with the radio. That I can do. It doesn't take too much of my energy.

Big J keeps interfering. He grabs the steering wheel and starts laughing. "Check it out, friend! I am getting good at this."

"Stop!" I try to get him away from the wheel. Here we are, still trying to keep him from bullying us. It never ends. The car swerves back and forth. Damian looks shaken. Selena knows we're here and is able to keep her cool.

As we get to the auto shop, Big J starts messing with the only light at the place. He places his arms up to it and it starts shaking and blinking on and off.

"Why are you doing this?" I yell at him.

"They're not going to hurt my family. That's what they're trying to do."

"Why would they do that? You're the ones always hurting us."

The light pops, and, now, it's pitch-black. Selena pulls out her cell phone and lights up the path, and they continue toward the back.

"Oh no you don't, Selena," Big J growls, following right behind her. Next, he tries to stop her from opening a window to climb into the auto shop. He's holding it shut, laughing, but I manage to lift his arms off the window, and it opens. They get inside. Wow! He's working extra hard to stop her. Again, once inside, he makes Selena's phone die.

"Why'd you do that?"

"I'm learning lots of things I can do. It's pretty cool."

Cris quickly gives her his phone, and I don't let him get close to my brother. Besides, he's depleted his energy. There's only so much you can use. We stand by as they discover the secret. We already knew about the third car. Big J leaves the building, pounding his own fist. I follow Cris, Damian and Selena to the house.

Cris

It's late now, and Mom must have fallen asleep. I don't see her in the living room or the kitchen. I stalk my way to her room but find her asleep with her work clothes still on. I slowly walk out and close the door. She must be exhausted.

An engine sounds, and a car's headlights shine through the window. Knocking on the door wakes Mom up and brings her into the living room, where Damian, Selena and I are sitting on the sofa. Selena is holding Lobo and talking to him as she pets his head and back. Stumbling to get to the door, I open it and see Felix standing in the night dew.

"Felix, what happened?" Mom asks.

I open the door wide so he can come in. Lobo jumps off Selena's lap, sniffs his boots and starts wagging his tail in a fast beat.

"Mamá, this is Selena, the girl I told you about. You better sit down. She has some news to share with us about the accident," I say.

Mom gives Selena a curious smile and sits down on the couch. "Selena, welcome to our home. What is it you know?"

Felix comes in and sits down on a chair in front of the sofa.

"*¿Quieres café*, Felix?" Mom asks.

"No, *gracias*, Mrs. Pérez. I want to know what these kids know."

Selena starts to explain what she knows about Sheriff Tanner, who has been trying to keep her mom and her away from Rico. "Jack Tanner for some reason wanted to hurt Rico and thought causing an accident to blame on him would be a solution. Rico has a white pickup like the one in the accident. Sheriff Tanner's pickup was white, but he painted it gray to cover it up. He's going to go after Rico, and he thinks he can get away with it because he's the sheriff."

"Rico's pickup is an older Chevy model. I know the truck," Felix says. "The sheriff's truck is a new Ford. They're completely different."

"It doesn't matter. He thinks he can frame Rico," Selena says.

"Can you prove this?" Felix asks at Selena.

She pulls out her phone and opens a video of Tanner at the auto shop talking to his friend about the accident.

"My mom and I were with him when he stopped at the shop. He was showing us the rental house he had because he wanted us to move in. No one knew I was recording them. I had to be careful and not let anyone know what I knew. I was just trying to find out what he was going to do. I'm sorry. I had no idea my family would do this. Honestly, I don't know them that well," she says. "I do think it was an accident.... I don't think he meant it to happen, not like it did. I knew you all would want to know as soon as possible. The third car caused it. I don't know if it was an accident or if it was intentional. All I know is it was my mom's friend. Whatever happens, I don't want Cris or his dad to be blamed."

Felix looks puzzled and reaches out to Selena. "What? Who could have wanted to do that? Do we know them? Who is your mom's friend?"

Selena bites her lip and looks at Felix straight in his eyes. "Unfortunately... you do. I'm sorry. My... he's... Mr. Tanner, the sheriff," Selena says, now in tears. "He's planning to take Rico in for questioning." Selena says, looking down at her feet.

"Not if I can help it," Felix states. "Can you send me that video?"

I pull out my cell phone. "Felix, I took pictures, too. Selena took us over to the auto shop earlier to show us the pickup. I'll send them to you."

Felix makes a disapproving face. "What the hell were you guys doing over there? That's dangerous."

I glance at Selena. "We were fine. It was kind of like superhero work."

"Y'all are not superheroes. Leave catching the bad guys up to us. I'll handle it from here," Felix says. "You three will need to stay out of this. Let us do the investigating. We'll find out what's going on, don't worry."

I look at Felix and say, "Please let me go with you to talk to my dad."

He shakes his head. "We're going to go by and give him a head's up and maybe question him. He hasn't been arrested. I'll let you know when you can talk to him. For now, please wait until I call you."

Lobo jumps up on my legs, and I reach down and scoop him up, petting the back of his head. I feel calmer.

"Nice pup," Felix says. "I'll call as soon as I can," he says and leaves.

"*¡Ay Diooooos mío!*" Mom suddenly screeches as she falls to the ground.

I quickly pick her up and set her down on the sofa. She's a nervous wreck.

"Mamá, it's going to be all right. Felix is going to help us. Don't worry," I say, trying to comfort her.

While she's reclining on the sofa with her head on my shoulder, Damian and Selena go into the kitchen and start moving dishes around. In a minute, they come back with hot cups of *té de manzanilla*.

"Here, Mrs. Pérez, drink some hot tea. You'll feel better. Do you want me to heat up a *tortilla* or do you want some toast?" Damian offers.

Mom hugs her drink. "No, Damian, the tea is enough. I'm fine. Selena, you did a brave thing. Thank you." Mom cradles her mug and holds it close to her chest, inhaling the aroma while she closes her eyes.

"I'm not sure what to think right now," Selena says tentatively. "I kept hearing a voice in my head telling me to help Cris and Rico. Strange things have been happening. I couldn't stand it anymore. My phone and car radio would randomly turn on and off. The lights in my room did the same. I felt like I was getting messages from someone."

"It's Carlos," I tell her. "He's been doing the same to me."

"I don't know Carlos," she says.

"Maybe not, but he obviously knows what's going on with all of us. He's trying to help us."

I grab Carlos' picture from the living room table and hand it to Selena. This is my brother. He's frozen in his frame, smiling as if he's happy we're talking about him.

"I've seen him," she says.

"When? You said you didn't know him."

"He was in my dream the other night. It seemed real. He came into my room, talked to me and told me to tell you what I knew," she says.

"Oh my God! Why didn't you tell me that before? He visited you?" I shout. "What did he say? What did he do? Tell me."

"Is that what you call it... a visit?" she says. "Well... my visit or dream was strange. He was standing at the foot of my bed, glowing with a bright light outlining him. He smiled and said, 'I've been wanting to talk to you. Do you know why I'm here?'"

Placing her hands over her heart, Selena continues, "I wasn't scared. I felt calm and at peace. I listened to him. He said he wanted me to find out about the accident. He said I would find the answers."

"Selena, he's my brother, my ghost brother. Yeah, he's visiting," I say.

"I think I better get back home. Do you need a ride, Damian?" Selena asks.

"Nah, I'll stay here, thanks."

With that, Selena bids us all goodbye, then scoops up Lobo and hugs and kisses him.

"I'll walk you out to the car," I offer.

Carlos

Cris walks Selena out to the car, and I have to admit I'm a bit nervous about the whole thing not working out. They now have the information they need to help Rico. The moon is shining brightly now, and how I wish I could fly away toward it. But I still have work to do.

"So, was it because of your mom's friend, Sheriff Tanner, or were you trying to ghost me. You know... after everything I've been through. I can take the truth. I've gotten pretty tough," Cris tells Selena.

"Oh my God, Cris! I swear, Sheriff Tanner freakin scares me. I had no choice. I didn't want to hurt you, really. I would never want to ghost you... well, at least I wouldn't mean to ghost you."

Changing the touchy subject, Cris says, "Nice ride."

"Yeah, it's really my mom's, but I get to drive it. She doesn't like to drive. We're working on our mother-daughter relationship. You know, therapy...."

"I wish my mom and I would do that. We do have my grandma, though. She helps. Hey, I better get back in and let you go. I'm sure Mom is wondering about everything that's happening. Your mom's probably worried, too."

"Did I do the right thing?" She tilts her head to the side. "You know, I imagine the sheriff will find out I was the one who talked to the police. What's going to happen with him, Mrs. Tanner and little Angie?"

"Selena, I know you're doing the right thing. We wouldn't be able to live with ourselves. We have to do what's right."

Cris places his hand on her shoulder and massages it a bit. "You'll let me know if you hear anything, right?"

"Of course. I'll call you as soon as I hear from Felix," Selena promises.

She gets in the car, and he closes the door for her. As she drives away, she watches him in the rearview mirror and waves in the darkness.

"Did his brother really think I could help, and did I really see him?" she says out loud to herself and starts laughing. "This is all so weird."

Cris

The weekend passes, and I lay low by staying home. I don't want to jinx anything, so I figure not talking to anyone is safe. I don't even call Damian. He texts me, and I don't answer him. I'm waiting to hear from Felix. Now, it's Monday morning, and I have to get ready for school.

I sit on my bed, staring at my phone. I dial Selena and she picks up immediately. "Don't go to school today. We have to figure out what we're going to do. Tell your mom you're sick, and I'll go pick you up later," I say.

Her voice lifts my spirits up. "You're going to get me into more trouble, but you're right. We do need to figure all of this out. Text me when you're on your way," she says.

I hang up and text Damian. My fingers are moving a hundred miles an hour and can't go as fast as my mind is going, "Hey, can't pick you up today... I have stuff to do. See you later."

I pull out my laptop and start researching stuff on Google. Before I know it, the morning has passed. I hear a knock on the front door, and Lobo starts barking. Mom shuffles toward the living room, and I run to beat her to the door.

I swing open the door and say, "Felix, I've been waiting to hear from you. Come in, please."

Felix takes off his hat and holds it in his hand. He walks into the living room and stands in front of the sofa. "Are you sick? Why aren't you in school? Anyway, we're investigating, and Sheriff Tanner will be brought in for questioning. We'll be bringing in the owner of the auto shop as well as Mrs. Tanner. We're just getting started," he says and looks at Mom.

Exhaling with relief, I ask, "What about Rico?"

Felix shuffles his feet and holds his hat tightly. "Rico has been cleared. You are free to talk to him anytime. Lillith and Selena too."

Pointing to the ceiling, "*¡Gracias a Dios!*" Mom blurts out and forms the sign of the cross on her head, heart and both shoulders, then kisses her hand raising it up to the ceiling.

Felix continues, "There's more. Apparently, Sheriff Tanner has been living some sort of double life."

I scoot up closer to him, hoping he'll say something about the sheriff being involved in some evil scheme. "Felix, does any of it involve *brujería*?"

Felix's eyes open wide, and he takes a step back, "What? Look… I don't know anything about witchcraft…." He scrunches his eyes and looks at me as if I'm crazy. "All I know is he may have been involved in some drug smuggling. The owner of the auto shop confessed to all sorts of illegal activity. He wanted a deal. The shed you kids went to is a front to cover everything up. As far as anything else… they're investigating. We'll let you know what we find out."

I slap my hand against my thigh. "I knew it! Something seemed off. That's why I'm getting all those messages." I blurt out.

Felix wrinkles his brow. "Messages? What do you mean?"

Holding onto my stomach, I sit down on the sofa. "Nothing, it's just weird. Thanks for letting us know, Felix. I think I need to throw up."

Felix places his hand on my shoulder. "Sorry I can't say anything else, Cris. I'm simply doing my job. If you need anything, call me. Oh… Cris, hold on, I do have something for you."

Felix excuses himself and heads back out to his car.

"I believe this is yours," he hands me Carlos' jacket. "Your dad asked me to give it to you. He wanted to make sure you got it."

I can't help but half-smile and grab the jacket. "Thanks, Felix, I don't know what we'd ever do if we lost this."

I place my hand over my heart and turn back to hug Mom, who has joined me at the door. We're feeling much better than we've felt for a while.

Felix nods. "Call if you need anything. I'll do my best to keep you both posted." He turns and leaves.

"Mamá, this is all good news. We can finally start over again. We have each other, and Carlos is with us." I hug her tightly as a gush of wind tousles our hair, and we close the front door.

At that moment, Carlos' picture crashes down to the floor and doesn't even crack. I look at Mom, reach over to pick up the picture and smile at him.

"No, brother, you're not dead, are you? You are here. You've been here the whole time."

"Mom, it may have been a miracle for me to have survived the crash, but Carlos is a miracle because he's my angel. He helped me find Dad, warned me and saved me from getting into some deep trouble. I know he'll always protect us. He's my ghost brother."

I rush to get dressed. Turning my stereo on as loud as possible, I slip on my old boots. I grab the notebook by my bed. "Today is the first day of my new life. Everything is going to be all right," I write. I put away the notebook and pen thinking I'll write more later.

I rush into the kitchen where Mom is moving around with much more rhythm. I grab the keys from the nail and kiss her goodbye.

"*Qué Dios te bendiga, m'ijito*," she says.

I run out the door and notice the ivy wrapping around the oak tree. It's bright green leaves have tripled in size and reach up to the top of the tree. The wind picks up and my hair lifts with the gusts as the leaves dance with their partners on the ground. I drive off in my old pickup truck as I dial Selena.

Carlos

Cris just called Selena, and he's coming to pick her up. Her mom is totally freaking out right now, not because of Cris but because of the phone call from Mrs. Tanner. I couldn't help hearing their conversation. The police arrested her husband, the sheriff, and they're raiding the auto shop right now. I don't know what Selena is going to do. She'll probably sneak out with Cris while her mom gets dressed. Cris' pickup drives up, and Selena runs outside to meet him.

"Oh my God, Cris! Did you hear the news?" she shouts while hopping into his pickup. "Hurry, before my mom sees you."

"I can't believe it." I say.

"Mrs. Tanner said they picked up the sheriff, and she was freaking out about him and the auto shop," Selena says, trembling.

"You didn't do anything wrong... don't worry. They're probably only going to question him." He tries to calm her.

"No, it's worse than that. He's not a good person. I know he's into some bad stuff. It was a matter of time."

They drive toward Rico's apartment.

"It's all right, Selena. My dad will know what to do."

They arrive, walk up the stairs and knock on his door.

He answers immediately. "Son, Selena, come in. I was on my way to the diner. What is it?"

"It's Sheriff Tanner," Cris says.

"He's my mom's friend," Selena adds.

"What about him?" Rico asks.

"The police took him in for questioning," Cris says.

"Things are finally catching up with him. Good," Dad says.

He goes into his kitchen and pours a glass of water from the sink and takes a drink. "Do you all want something to drink? I have coffee," he offers.

"No, thanks, but what should we do? What should Selena do? Her mom is upset with her."

"Don't worry about Lillith. I'll talk to her. She'll be fine. It's for the best. He was only hurting her. He never let her live her life," Rico says. "Even when your uncle Carlos, my brother, was here, he was always trying to get her away from him. I don't know what his problem is, what hold he has on her."

"That's how he is with me," Selena says. "He tries to control everything I do. Mom listens to him. Rico, I need to ask you. It never mattered to me before. But, now with Cris and all… Was Carlos my dad?" Selena asks.

Cris steps back. "Woahhhh… He can't be. Right, Dad?"

"Selena, your mom never wanted you to know who your dad was, and I always respected that, but now everything is different. I think you need to talk to her. She needs to tell you. Do you want me to go with you?" Rico says.

"Yes, Rico, please come with me. She won't listen to me, especially now."

"Wait a minute, shouldn't you both be in school?"

"We have more important things to do today," Selena and Cris say at the same time.

"Fine, let's go see Lillith."

Cris

We head to Selena's house, and I think I'm more nervous than her. She sits quietly in Rico's Mustang as we drive along.

"Selena, there's one question I wanted to ask you before you find out about your dad," I say.

"What is it, Cris?"

"What were you doing that night in the cemetery when Damian and I saw you dancing by my uncle's grave?"

"Oh my God, Cris! I was just dancing. I love to express myself, you should know that. My mom wanted to live near the cemetery to be close to him... so she could talk to him."

"Okay." I answer, somewhat relieved.

"The kids are from my mom's group. We were practicing.... If you don't know by now, my mom is kinda... you know, kinda weird."

"All parents are weird, I guess, in a way."

"I'm not a witch, at least not that kind. I guess we have a lot to learn about each other, if you want to."

Selena smiles as she gets out of the car and heads to her house with Rico and me following.

"Yep, we have a lot to figure out," I say.

Selena unlocks the front door and lets us in. "Go ahead and sit down. I'll go find my mom."

We sit in the living room with the lingering smell of cigarette smoke. The smell is making me sneeze. I'm not used to it. I don't know how Selena stands it. My allergies can't handle it. The house is cold, even though it's warm outside, and it's dark, even though the sun is bright.

Selena walks in. "She's coming," she says, fixing her smeared mascara, as if she's been crying, and sits down across from Rico and next to me.

Lillith walks in with red, swollen eyes. She sits down next to Rico.

"Selena says you need to talk to me," she says.

"Lillith, are you all right?" Rico asks her.

"Rico, everything is going wrong for me. Lilly doesn't understand."

"Yes, she does. That's why we're here. Listen, all this concerns, Lilly. Her future matters to you, right? She needs to know who her father is," Rico goes straight to the point.

"What? No! She doesn't need to know. It doesn't matter."

"Tell her, Lillith. She thinks it's Carlos."

Lillith stands up with her hand on her forehead and starts crying out loud. "You know I loved Carlos, I always will. What was I supposed to do? Jack Tanner came to tell me about what had happened, and he said he'd take care of me. I needed him. Carlos was gone. What could I do?"

"Who, Mom? Who said that?"

Lillith cries harder and louder. "Our friend, Lilly. He's much more than a friend, but you knew that, right?"

"What friend? What are you saying?"

"He's from my church. He's always been around and looked out for us. We told you he was a close friend to keep him in your life. He wanted to stay close by. Lilly… he's your father. He didn't want Mrs. Tanner to find out. I guess now she and everyone will know."

"What? What the... Oh my GOD, Mom! What are you saying?" Selena yells, turns and runs out of the room.

Lillith tries to run after her, but Rico rushes in front of her, gently holding her back.

"Give her a minute. She'll come back."

Only whimpers break the silence of the smoky room. After a few minutes, Selena is back.

"He's my father? All this time I thought I didn't have a father, and he was right in front of me. What were you thinking? Now he's probably going to jail or maybe even prison. Wow, unbelievable! Did you think I'd never find out? For goodness sake, Mom! I hate you right now! Do you know I really hate you so much right now?!!"

Selena starts pacing back and forth, throwing her head up in the air, staring at the ceiling. I try to place my hand on her shoulder, but she won't stay still.

"Thank you, Lillith," Rico says. "I know that must have been hard for you. She had to know, and she doesn't hate you."

"Let's go, Cris. I need to get out of here," Selena says, grabbing her purse and keys.

We both rush out the door.

We get in the sports car and drive off toward the outskirts of Malton. We drive past the auto shop. Sunshine is breaking through the clouds as they shapeshift across the clear sky. Selena reaches over and turns on the radio. It automatically shuts off. She looks at me.

"Is that you, brother? Or is it the other guy?"

"What other guy?"

"They've both been sort of giving me messages." She swallows. "J."

"J? You mean Big J?" I ask while looking at the radio.

"Yep, once a jerk, always a jerk. The worst part is all this time I've been related to him and never knew it. I don't think he did either."

"You can hear both of them? My brother and the mean dude? Wow! I can't believe it. I wonder if Carlos knows. I think he's been trying to help us the whole time. He had to know."

Selena pulls over. Some of the cattle roaming in the pastures look our way. We step out of the car and lean against the door and observe the beautiful, peaceful scene. I put my arms around Selena.

"Do you want to see him?" I ask.

"Who?"

"Your dad," I say.

She nods. "You'd think I wouldn't want to, but I can't help it. I have so many questions for him. I want to yell at him at the top of my lungs and scream hateful words, but I also want to hug him and tell him I have always wanted a father."

She starts crying and I hold her. Her tears dampen my faded T-shirt, and for once I sort of understand her.

"Your feelings are valid," I say. "Maybe he did what he thought he had to do. Everyone makes mistakes. You can still give him a chance to be your dad."

She takes a breath and nods. "I want to see him. Will you call Felix and take me to him?"

We head back to town, and Felix is waiting for us outside the police station. Selena takes a deep breath, and we step out of the vehicle.

"He's been asking for you," Felix tells Selena.

As Felix escorts Selena in to see Sheriff Jack Tanner, I sit down on one of the metal chairs in the lobby and wait. I stare at the plain concrete floor and tap my foot against the edge of the chair. I sit in silence, glancing up occasionally to see if Selena is returning. Finally, a door opens, and she comes out, wearing a half-smile. That's a good sign, I think. I get up to greet her.

"I feel so much better," she says. "He'll be getting out on bail, and we'll be able to talk about everything. It's not how they made it sound. I believe him. He wanted to protect me and Big J. Now, he's going to have to accept you, I told him.... And he's worried about my mom."

We stand up and walk out of the police station into the warm sunshine.

Selena asks me to drive. I take the keys from her. We're off in the white sports car. I feel much lighter. I can breathe easier, and my future seems much brighter.

"Will you do me a favor, Cris?"

"Sure."

"Do you mind stopping by a friend's place for me? I need to drop something off."

We drive downtown to an apartment close to the diner.

"Here," she says, jumps out and opens the trunk. "I'll be right back." She's holding a small suitcase as she climbs up the front stairs. I can see her knocking on the door. The door opens. It looks like Angélica, the waitress from the diner. Selena stands there, talking to her, then hugs her and hands her the suitcase. Then she runs down the stairs smiling and jumps into the car.

Selena leans over and messes with the radio as I start to drive away.

"Are you all right?" I ask.

She sits back and looks out the window at some children playing outside. "I'm great," she answers.

Taking hold of her hand, I slow down as I approach a stop sign. "Sorry for asking, but that's the waitress, right?"

"Yeah, she works at the diner with Rico. She's my friend. Do you know her?"

Still at the stop sign, I turn to get Selena's full attention. "No, not really… but she knows about Carlos."

Selena starts laughing. "Yeah, she's gifted. She's been mentoring me."

I squint my eyes in confusion. "Well, she told me Carlos wanted me to stay away from you… that you were into weird stuff."

I take off and keep driving. "Well, she was probably trying to protect me. She's like a big sister, you know, but she's good at what she does. Maybe not a full-blown *curandera*, but she does know her stuff for sure. Now everything is out in the open, right?"

We approach the house and I park the car.

"So, what was in the suitcase?" I ask.

"Some old stuff I don't think I need anymore. Angélica lent it to me for research, but I think I'll stick to my instincts. I'm good."

I turn off the car and unbuckle my seatbelt. "It's a good time to move forward and leave some of our past behind. Forgiveness is not easy, especially when we've been through so much."

Selena opens her car door. "I've already forgiven them. Now I need to talk to my mom. It's like I'm in one of those corny movies with a title like, 'Everything my mom kept from me.' No matter, I still love her. We'll make it work."

"I know you will. I'm so glad Rico was able to help. He's a great guy. Hopefully, he'll be coming around now, too."

We get out of the car, go inside my home and step into the living room.

I tell Selena, "Well, I know the hardest part is forgiving myself, but I'm ready to move forward."

Selena spins around with her arms extended and her eyes closed. "I see him," she says. "He's here. He's standing next to his altar. Talk to him, Cris."

I approach the lit candles, burning brighter than I've ever seen them before, and say, "Carlos, if you can hear me, I'm sorry. I know it wasn't my fault, and I forgive everyone, even Big J. Please tell him. I love you, brother. Thanks for helping me. I couldn't have figured all of this out without you."

Selena smiles. "He says not to worry about him. He's fine. And he knows you and your mom will be fine, too."

"Carlos, I don't want you to leave, but I know you can't stay here. It's selfish of me to keep you here."

Selena gently squeezes my hand and closes her eyes. "He loves you and your mother and will always be with you. Pay attention to unexpected messages. He'll always communicate with you."

The brightest light shines in through the window and illuminates the entire living room for a split second. As we peek outside, we see our world come to life.

No, my brother is not dead. He's in me, in my family, in our home, in the ivy I planted, in the cardinal that visits my window, in my dog Lobo and in my music. He lives in the life I'm living now. I stare at his picture surrounded by candles propped up on the living room coffee table. "C... I feel you, brother." I hold his picture up as the light shines on it. He smiles back at me, forever frozen. I can finally say I'm happy. I'm genuinely happy.

I place him back onto his makeshift altar and pull out my cell phone. I need to call Damian. I have so much to tell him, and it's not on social media, at least not yet.

ACKNOWLEDGEMENTS

It has been a long journey since I wrote the first sentence of the initial draft of this book. This project began more than six years ago when I started writing bits and pieces; then I'd put it away. I wanted to write a story about someone who passed away and could communicate with their family because these experiences were personal to me after losing my sister. I began talking to my mom about the idea of the two brothers. She believed in receiving messages from our loved ones who had passed. We talked about it all the time. We would share stories about visits from the other side, cardinals, dreams and spiritual experiences.

After losing my mom unexpectedly and a year later my dad, writing a book about the possibilities of life after death meant so much more to me. Especially now, so many people have felt the loss of a loved one and are comforted by the hope of life after death. We pray that there is more beyond this life.

By utilizing alternating points of view, both brothers, living and dead, are heard. A voice from the other side offers readers hope their relationship with a loved one continues after death. I believe it is a hope we all have. It is a comfort we all yearn for.

Above anyone, I thank God for allowing me this opportunity. Thank you to my parents, Joe V. Sanchez and Elida Reyna Sanchez, for always inspiring, supporting, guiding, believing in and loving me unconditionally. Thank you also to my loving family: my husband, Richard, sons and daughters-in-law, Ricky and Jessica, Joseph and Jackie, Matthew, Lucas, and my four beautiful grandchildren, who have brought joy to all my family's lives and given us so much hope for a brighter future. My family understands the work I am passionate about and my beliefs about life after death. They have always supported me, read my work, listened to me read to them, helped me proofread and been extremely patient. They have heard me talking about Carlos, Cris, Selena and Damian for years as if they were real kids.

Thank you to my sister Ana for continuing to inspire me. And thank you to my siblings, Joe, Nina, Obie and George, who have always encouraged me. I'm grateful to my younger sister for never saying no when I asked for last-minute advice or edits. Thank you to all my in-laws for loving me like their own family. Thank you also to all my extended *familia: mis tías, tíos, primos, primas, sobrinos, sobrinas, amigas y amigos* for being in my life. I am blessed to be surrounded by all of them.

I would also like to thank Arte Público for welcoming me into their literary *familia*. I greatly appreciate their knowledge and insight into bringing *Ghost Brother* to life. I am grateful they saw something in my story and believed in me and our Mexican-American culture. Their belief in my work has motivated me to grow as a writer. I am truly humbled and honored.

May God continue to bless everyone.